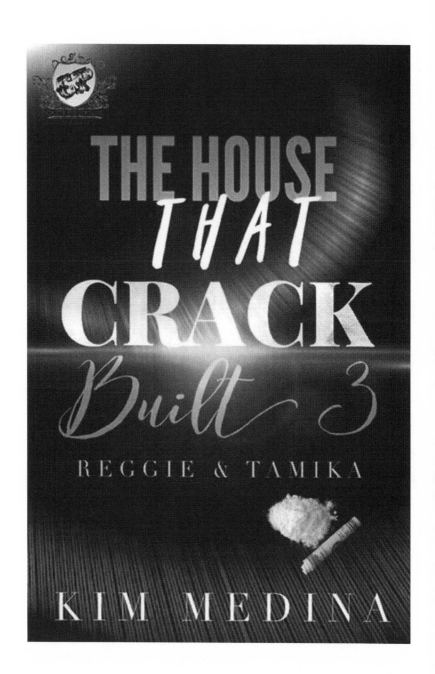

THE HOUSE
THAT
CRACK
Built 3

REGGIE & TAMIKA

KIM MEDINA

BY KIM MEDINA

Check out other titles by The Cartel Publications

4   BY KIM MEDINA

THE HOUSE THAT CRACK BUILT 3:

Reggie & Tamika

BY

KIM MEDINA

Library of Congress Control Number: 2017963028

ISBN 10: 1945240989

ISBN 13: 978-1945240980

Cover Design: Cover Design: Bookslutgirl.com

www.thecartelpublications.com
First Edition
Printed in the United States of America

What's Up Fam,

It's almost Christmas!! This is the best time of the year to me. I love the lights, the music and especially the Christmas movies. There is nothing better than sitting in the dark with nothing but the Christmas lights on and listening to, "Christmas Interpretations" by Boyz II Men. I pray that you have love and everything your heart desires this and every year.

Ok, so onto the moment we've all been waiting for..."The House That Crack Built 3"! This novel is incredible! I personally think it's the best of the entire series so far! I mean, the drama, is kicked up to a whole new notch! So hold onto your hats and get ready for a great read!

With that being said, keeping in line with tradition, we want to give respect to a vet or trailblazer paving the way. In this novel, we would like to recognize:

Jenifer Lewis

Jenifer Jeanette Lewis is an American actress, comedian, singer, activist and now author who

BY KIM MEDINA

first got her start on Broadway in musicals. She was also backup singer for Bette Midler prior to her acting roles in major motion pictures. In addition to starring in the hit TV show, "Black-ish", she has penned a memoir entitled, "Jenifer Lewis: The Mother of Black Hollywood". As someone who has made over 300 appearances for film, TV and stage, Jenifer Lewis is clearly and expert in life and shares her experiences, highs and lows with the world. Make sure you check it out!

Aight, get to it. I'll catch you in the next book.

Be Easy!

Charisse "C. Wash" Washington
Vice President
The Cartel Publications
www.thecartelpublications.com
www.facebook.com/publishercwash
Instagram: publishercwash
www.twitter.com/cartelbooks
www.facebook.com/cartelpublications
Follow us on Instagram: Cartelpublications
#CartelPublications

#UrbanFiction

#PrayForCeCe

#JeniferLewis

BY KIM MEDINA

CARTEL URBAN CINEMA'S 3rd WEB SERIES

BMORE CHICKS

@ Pink Crystal Inn

NOW AVAILABLE:

Via

YOUTUBE

And

DVD

(Season 2 Coming in January)

www.youtube.com/user/tstyles74

www.cartelurbancinema.com

www.thecartelpublications.com

MOTHER MONSTER

The movie based off the book,

"RAUNCHY"

by

T. Styles

Now Available on You Tube

Available to Download via VIMEO

www.cartelurbancinema.com and

www.thecartelpublications.com

BY KIM MEDINA

CARTEL URBAN CINEMA'S 2nd WEB SERIES

IT'LL COST YOU (Twisted Tales Season One)

NOW AVAILABLE:
YOUTUBE / STREAMING / DVD

www.youtube.com/user/tstyles74
www.cartelurbancinema.com
www.thecartelpublications.com

THE HOUSE THAT CRACK BUILT 3   13

CARTEL URBAN CINEMA'S 1st WEB SERIES

THE WORST OF US (Season One & Season Two)

NOW AVAILABLE:
YOUTUBE / STREAMING/ DVD

www.youtube.com/user/tstyles74
www.cartelurbancinema.com
www.thecartelpublications.com

BY KIM MEDINA

CARTEL URBAN CINEMA'S 1st MOVIE

PITBULLS IN A SKIRT – THE MOVIE

www.cartelurbancinema.com and

www.amazon.com

www.thecartelpublications.com

#TheHouseThatCrackBuilt3

BY KIM MEDINA

PROLOGUE

*T*amika stood in the middle of a crowd of eager men. Carmelo, the groom, excitedly rubbed the sweat from his palms as he anticipated the cutie blessing his lap with a dance. Besides, for the past few months everyone had been talking about the girl who could move her body like a snake and seeing as though he would be a married man in a few days, he wanted to share his moment with her.

When the bass from 'Bodak Yellow' thumped through the speakers, Tamika swirled her hips and waist as if it would twist off at any moment. She wanted him to know she was with it all. She could feel Carmelo's eyes on her and could even see the fresh stiffness rising in his pants. Carefully she moved toward him before sitting on his lap. Once situated, she pushed and twirled into him as if he were her husband.

"Don't move, sexy," he said in her ear, his breath tart from too much drinking. "I'ma 'bout to bust and you feel so fucking good. Damn, man."

She continued to dance on him but said, "I don't mind all that, but you gotta give my brother over there extra before you let loose, otherwise it's just the dance." She moved to get up and he forcefully put her back into his lap, waving Drillo over quickly.

"What you need, man?" Drillo said into his ear, to be heard over the music.

"Extra," Carmelo said, reaching into his pocket, handing Drillo a fifty. "I'ma need that to happen."

Having seen the exchange, his friends cheered him on excitedly knowing he was about to risk it all. "You got that, but you don't want yours off now right?" Drillo said as Tamika continued to work as he handled the money part of the business. "Meet us in the room in about ten minutes."

Carmelo glared. "Alright, but don't be fuckin' with my money. It wouldn't be good for your life."

"Ain't nobody messing with you, man," Drillo said. "This your night." He slapped him on the back and Tamika got up.

"Hurry up because I'ma be waiting," she said winking at him. "I'm going into the bathroom to freshen up."

She and Drillo rushed into the bathroom and grabbed the clothes she stashed in the tub. Next she quickly slipped into her jeans and white t-shirt. For the night they had already collected $450,

BY KIM MEDINA

courtesy of her dancing skills and now it was time to bounce.

While Carmelo's friends poured tequila down his throat in celebration for the upcoming nuptials, Tamika and Drillo slipped out the house, breaking the future deal and escaping with the tips and $50.00 additional bucks. Thirty minutes later they copped from their regular dealer and was getting high in a run down motel room in Baltimore City.

Sitting on the edge of the bed, next to the curtains, Tamika grabbed the lighter from her purse to get high.

"Hurry the fuck up," Drillo said sitting next to her. "You taking too long."

"Calm down!" Tamika scolded him. "This from me dancing not you."

The moment she ignited the lighter, a huge flame flew from it and connected to the curtain by her head. Within seconds the material went up in flames along with Tamika's braids. As she dropped the pipe to slap at her face and arms, in an effort to put out the fire, Drillo picked up the pipe attempting to smoke.

Searing pain took over her body and before long she was engulfed.

CHAPTER ONE

REGGIE

6 MONTHS EARLIER

My wife was an addict.

And as much as I hated to admit it, it was mostly my fault. All she ever wanted to do was love me and at one point in my life I couldn't see giving her what she needed. The past, and wanting to build a relationship with my moms was all that my mind was on at the time. And now I was feeling like it was too late for me to make things right. And keep the promise I made to her mother.

I just picked her up from the rehab place after she completed a six-month program. She looked healthy and I hoped that was true. "You hungry?" I asked.

She smiled, reached over and put her hand on my leg. "To be honest I was hoping you'd scoop me up with something fried." She laughed. "I haven't eaten anything good in months."

"My bad, bae. I guess I was just so excited about getting to you that I wasn't using my head."

BY KIM MEDINA

She smiled. "Reggie, I can tell you worried but I don't want you to be. I'm seriously done with drugs. I mean, I hated the idea of me not being in your life with everything going on with Russo not walking and Amina having to take care of them. How are they anyway?"

I took a deep breath. "You know what, I'ma let you find that out for yourself."

RUSSO

I'm not sure but I swear I think my wife is trying to kill me. Earlier she was supposed to be giving me a bath but I been in this bitch for over an hour. Done pissed five times and felt like I had to shit too. This can't be my life.

FUCK!

I don't know what's on her mind but lately she had been treating me badly. Like I did something to her. And every time I asked what the problem was she'd claim nothing was wrong. Why the games?

When the bathroom door opened Amina came inside. "Bae, where were you? The water cold as fuck and—"

"You said you wanted to wash up alone so I gave you privacy." She said with an attitude.

I took a deep breath. "Amina, I didn't mean it that way. I just meant that you do so much that—"

"Nah, what you are is an ungrateful ass nigga who don't appreciate shit I do around here." She frowned. "I pick up behind you." She tossed up her arms. "Cook for you. Clean your fucking pamper and what do I get in return? Complaints! Well I'm sick of your shit!"

See what I'm saying? She kirking out for no reason.

"Amina, can you calm down a—"

"Fuck a calm down! If you think life is so sweet without me then live fast nigga because I'm not taking no more of this shit." She reached down, turned on the cold water.

"What you doing?" I yelled.

Before I could say anything more she turned the shower on, the ice water slapping against my face. "I'ma leave you in here to cool the fuck off!"

She stomped toward the door and walked out.

I tried to scoot towards the front of the tub to turn off the shower but couldn't reach it. Everything was slippery.

"AMINA! COME BACK!"

TAMIKA

He had taken me to Rusty Scupper and I couldn't believe how romantic this place was. Low lights. Elegant silverware. And because it was nighttime we were staring out on the water, the lights from the building causing everything to glow.

"So talk to me," he said. "How was it being there?"

"You really want to do this?" I asked biting a piece of my crab cake. "Over dinner, Reggie?"

He nodded. "I figured you would talk to me a little more about it now because when it came up in the past you were kinda quiet. Like you were trying to forget about it so I left you to it."

I took a deep breath. "Reggie, I was using drugs and I almost lost my husband. What's there to talk about?" I shrugged. "I want to forget it all."

"That part ain't true," he said sipping his Hennessey and coke.

"What part?"

"The part about losing me." He paused. "I told you before and I'll say it again, I had no intentions on leaving you, Tamika. I just wanted you to get better so we could have the life we deserved."

I took a deep breath. "I don't know. I guess being in there made me realize how important being out here was to me. You don't know what it's like until you can't walk around and do, eat and go where you want to." I paused. "It had me fucked up mentally."

He shook his head. "I'm sorry."

"I know. And I forgive you." I ate some of my green beans. "So, have you talked to your mother?"

"Fuck no." He glared.

"Wow. Where's that coming from?"

"You serious?" His nostrils widened and closed. "Tamika, she was the reason you got so stressed that you started to use." He said pointing into the table.

24 BY KIM MEDINA

"Nah, I learned that whatever I went through was my fault and that I can't put that on another person."

"All the same." He shook his head. "We didn't have any problems before she came into the picture."

"And we won't have any now, Reggie," I smiled. "Relax a little. You the one who wanted to bring up the past."

He shook his head and smiled. "Now I see why you didn't wanna talk about that shit."

When his phone rung again, the fourth time for the night, he looked over at it, pressed a few keys and sat it face down. "You can answer the phone if you want."

"I know." He picked up his fork.

"Well why don't you?"

He shook his head and dropped the fork. "I haven't been able to be with my wife alone in months and you asking me that?"

I shrugged. "It just seems a little suspicious that's all."

He laughed and covered his mouth. "There my wife go." He said slyly. "At first I thought you were gonna fake like you were so perfect. I was fearing our situation would be boring but leave it to you to be on that jealous shit already," he joked.

"So you like that we argue?" I frowned.

"Nah, it ain't that. It's just that...well...before you went in you wanted to talk and I convinced myself that by not talking about shit things would go smoothly between us."

"And now?"

"And now I'm realizing that if we don't talk about it, the only thing that happens is that shit simmers and then blows up in our faces. And I don't want that," he said.

I nodded. "Okay, well let me get some things off my chest."

"I'm listening." Reggie wiped the corners of his mouth with the black cloth napkin.

"I hate you for making me go. I hate you for not coming to get me when I wanted to come back home. And I hate that you look well when my life felt like it was falling apart."

"Tamika, I didn't—"

"Nah, you wanted to hear the truth here it is!" I yelled, causing a few people to look at us. "You were supposed to be my hero. The man who was there for me even at my worst and you abandoned me, Reggie. To deal with things alone."

"Tamika, that's not how it went." He paused. "Yes I allowed my mother into the picture but I didn't know how to save an addict. And I was afraid to lose you."

"But you didn't even try."

"I DID TRY!" He roared, even louder than he had been moments earlier. "Remember? It wasn't you but I tried to save my mother and what did that get me? Nothing! And I wasn't willing to have the same thing happen to you, that's why I didn't pick you up when you begged to come home. We needed professional help. But don't for one second believe that for months I didn't have to drink myself to bed just to be able to shut my eyes. I fucking love you! But I couldn't see being with you how you were. Don't you get that?"

I nodded. "Yeah. I think so."

"I hope that's true, Tamika."

I took a deep breath. "Okay, so who was that on your phone?"

"Nobody." He grabbed his drink and took a sip.

"That's odd. Because I didn't think nobody's knew how to make a phone call."

"Okay, it's one of the few customers that Russo got left." He paused. "I'm taking care of things for him. You know with the feds sniffing around we can't move much weight so things have been tight. Funds are also low."

"And you bring me here? To an expensive restaurant?"

"Nothing but the best for my wife. So I saved up for this night."

I smiled. "Reggie, I love you, I really do. But we can't let anybody into our marriage again. Because although I wanna be strong, I'm nothing without you. I hope you understand what I'm saying."

"I do."

"Then save me from myself this time around. I'm begging you."

CHAPTER TWO
REGGIE

When I rolled over on the bed my wife wasn't beside me. Lately Tamika had been out the bed earlier than me and when I'd ask her where she was she'd tell me gone. But as always my dick was rock hard and I needed to relieve myself before I did the wrong thing. The best option would be my wife but like I said, she wasn't there.

Grabbing my shit, I stroked it a few times as I thought about the things I used to every time I wanted to get off. A big fat woman, with mounds of flesh, sucking me off with whip cream on my dick. Yeah it was a bit much but it always hit the spot when I wanted to get off quick.

After relieving the pressure, I wiped my hands and took a shower. And after getting dressed, I was about to head out to get on with life when I heard Russo calling out.

"Somebody, please help!" he yelled.

I stopped where I was, doubled back and walked passed his bedroom door. But when I entered the room I didn't see anybody. It took him calling out again for me to see him on the other side of the bed, half naked, in an adult diaper and on the floor.

"Damn, man, what happened to you?" I asked.

"Help me up," Russo begged.

When I lifted him and put him back on the bed I could smell the shit stemming from the diaper he wore. Now you gotta hear me when I say this. Russo my man, but I can't see changing him. I just can't. "Smells like you got a situation," I said frowning.

Russo looked down. "Fuck all that, I gotta tell you something, Reg."

"Shoot."

"I think my wife hates me or something."

I laughed heavily. "How the fuck you sound when that woman loves you as hard as she do? Think about it. How many women would've rolled out if you'd ended up like this?"

"I hear what you saying but still." He continued. "It's like I did something to her that she not trying to tell me."

I sat on the edge of the bed. "Well play the tapes back. What happened before you ended up in this chair that could have her acting crazy? Keep in mind I'm not saying that she is."

Russo scratched his head. "Man, I don't know. The last thing I remembered before I was shot was that we had made a promise to work things out...and now."

"Maybe you should talk to her."

"That's what I been doing. But like I said she not receiving me. Every time I bring it up she claims that shit cool. If that be the case then why she turning cold water on me in the tub and then pushing me off the bed with her feet?"

I covered my mouth, trying to hold in my laugh. "She kicked you off this bitch?"

"It's not funny, man!"

"I know, I know," I said extending my hands. "And I wish I knew what to tell you. I mean, I'm going through problems with Tamika so I'm the last one to claim experience with these sisters."

Russo shook his head. "I get it, well thanks for listening anyway."

I got up and walked out, just as Amina was coming inside.

AMINA

When Reggie left I could tell by the look in his eyes that they were talking about me. I could care less because at the end of the day I was going to do what I was going to do.

Walking over to the drawer I removed the adult sized diaper and the wipes. Sliding back over to the bed I flopped on it, grabbed his legs so that he was flat on his back and snatched off the tabs from his soggy pamper. All the while he was looking at me.

"Do you hate me, Amina?" He asked. "I mean, I don't know what it must be like to have to change your husband's pamper but, if you would tell me and be honest at least I'd know where you're coming from. This shit is killing me."

I chuckled. "So that's what you think this is about, Russo?"

"What else can I believe?"

"Maybe it's the fact that you don't appreciate me. Like I keep saying over and over. Why can't that be the reason?"

"I do appreciate you. And if I could spoil you how I use to then you would see."

I laughed.

"What's so funny?" He asked.

"Everything is about the dollar with you." I snatched out a few baby wipes, pushed his legs toward his face and wiped the brown shit from his butthole. I can't believe this is my life now.

"Well I did use to spend money on you. And with this case pending and me being fake broke I—,"

"Fake broke," I repeated. "You said that before and now I wanna know what it means? Because right now I gotta collect welfare to feed me and your daughter."

"Amina, please! You went down there yourself, talking about you didn't want nothing from me."

"If you stashing money around this bitch, now is the time to tell me. Because a bitch needs it now more than ever."

He took a deep breath. "I ain't got no money. Not what I use to. But I am able to scratch up something if I have to."

"Then stop saying that you fake broke and shit." I paused. "Because it's putting an insult on the fact that I had to apply for free lunch for Naverly."

"That was your choice too." He paused. "I'm not gonna be on my dick for long, Amina. Just stay with me and—"

I sealed up the fresh diaper he was wearing and picked up the other soiled one. "Work on how to be an honest fucking man." I tossed the dirty pamper in his face, his own shit smacking against his lips. "Let's start there." I stormed out.

CHAPTER THREE

REGGIE

When I pulled up in front of the house in a suburban area I looked at my Apple watch twice before the door opened and she walked toward my car. Leaning through the passenger side window she smiled in at me, as waving behind her.

"Took you long enough, nigga. I was starting to think that you set me up once again."

I shook my head. "You gonna talk or get in? 'Cause I got somewhere to be later. Plus you know my wife back home."

"I already know, nigga" She rolled her eyes and opened the door.

I drove about fifteen minutes before she finally said a word. Personally I had nothing to say. Our situation was one of convenience and she knew that, at least I hoped so. But I could feel her looking over at me every so often but I hated what was sometimes necessary to get her to do what I wanted. She loved a good fight before sex every time.

"How is everything?" She asked. "And before you say it, no I'm not trying to get into your business."

I smiled before glancing down at the GPS, which indicated how long we had before we reached the motel.

"So now you don't wanna talk?" She continued.

"What you want me to say, Tamara?" I shrugged. "Because for real, I ain't never been the talking type of dude."

She looked away and laughed hard. "You know, when I saw you at the gas station that day something told me not to approach you." She shook her head.

"But you did anyway." I leaned back and continued to steer the car.

She shrugged. "I could never understand why I like more of the same. I mean Russo did me wrong and even shot me and now you doing me just like him."

I laughed softly.

"Fuck is so funny?" She yelled.

"Look, do you wanna do this or not?"

"I wouldn't be here if I didn't."

"Then what difference does it make how we treat you? You offered your body for comfort to my man and me. Now he didn't want the pussy, but I do. The question is are you gonna change up or not and start acting all serious?"

"What about what I want?"

"What do you want?" I asked harshly. "Far as I know we don't stop our situation until you satisfied sexually too. What else could I possibly do for you at this point?"

"What if I wanted more?"

"Be specific."

"Like a relationship." She said. "What is so wrong with me that men only see me for one thing? Is it my face? My body? I mean what is it, Reggie?"

"Come on, man." I said waving at her with all that dumb shit. "We both know it's not your body."

"How would I know?" She said louder. "I mean nobody ever kept it real with me."

I took a deep breath and leaned back in my seat, before turning the radio off altogether. It played softly in the background, barely audible for real, but for some reason it started to annoy me. "When you stepped to me you said you understood my situation. Said you got how a man could be so confused by it all that he would slide outside his marriage every now and again."

"And I do," she said.

"Do you really?" I paused. "Because I'm starting to believe that was just a game to get a nigga where you wanted. Or where you thought you wanted."

"But I—"

"I'ma tell you something real," I said cutting her off. "Because if you were my daughter I'd want her to hear the same. You can't offer a man sand and then ask him to build a castle with you. They don't last."

"So my body's sand?"

"Basically."

"But if...if I," she looked out the window and took a deep breath. "I'm afraid if I don't lead with what I know...what I can give...you won't be around."

"I can't be around, Tamara," I said honestly. "I'm taken! Why I gotta keep telling you that?"

"But you here with me."

"That's right." I paused. "I got an addiction. I fucks when shit is on my mind. But my wife was the first person I didn't have sex with for over a

38   BY KIM MEDINA

year until I was sure. That means she's the one, not you."

Tamara's hands balled up and I could tell she was about to trip out.

"We ain't gonna make it to the motel are we?" I asked.

She shook her head no.

I pulled over and parked. "Look, I'm sorry I—"

She spit in my face and yanked the door to try and make a beeline to escape. Instead I snatched her hair, pulled down my zipper and forced her face toward my dick. She faked like she didn't want to suck it but that's how she got off. Fighting and shit.

Tamara didn't want a nigga to wife her. She wanted a nigga to make her feel anger. The prettiest thing you ever saw, she was tired of men telling her about her beauty. She wanted to be conscious of something down in her soul and that's how we worked.

Yes it was foul that she took care of Russo sexually before he shot her and got rid of her. And yes I was a married man. But at the end of the day my heart still belonged to Tamika, no matter what we went through. I just needed a nasty bitch every now and again.

"Suck that shit you dirty whore," I said as she pushed further on my shit, my thickness resting in her throat.

I didn't even have to hold her head anymore. She was like a robot, going to work because she was programmed to do so. I leaned my head back, before turning to the left to look out the window.

I closed my eyes.

Cars whizzed back and forth none knowing that I was being taken care of the way I was. When I glanced down I could tell she was in her comfort zone and thank God I was in mine.

CHAPTER FOUR

TAMIKA

I sat on the sofa, calm mostly, warm also, waiting on Reggie to come back. It had been over six hours since he left and I couldn't wait to see him. Besides, Russo was sleeping the last I checked and Amina was upstairs with Naverly doing homework. That meant all the time in the world for me and mine.

After what felt like forever, Reggie came inside and tossed his keys on the table by the door. "Hey, bae." He looked around where he stood. "What you doing up?"

"You mean what I'm doing up waiting for my husband who I slept without for months? In rehab and now I need to spend all the time I can."

He smiled and walked over to me, flopping on the sofa. "I love how you get my shit together."

I giggled. "Do you really? Because I'm home now and that means a lot more of that." I eased on top of him and looked into his eyes. "Tell me, Mr. Man. Where you been?"

He took a deep breath and I could smell alcohol. Right away I wanted a drink so I kissed his lips, hoping I could get a buzz. "Well, I could tell you stories of a night gone bad but I won't bore you to death," he said.

I giggled. "Please do. I need the entertainment. I mean, they got the same shows on with the same stories."

He chuckled and situated his dick before placing his hands on my waist. "Well, I had to see a few dudes for Russo in Southeast D.C. and then I got mad as fuck when I stepped outside and saw some clowns sitting on my car."

"What? Oh my, God baby. What you do?"

"You don't even wanna know." He rubbed his fingers and I could see the gashes.

"You gotta stop doing that."

"Doing what?"

"Hitting people with your bare hands. This is the day of HIV and all other kinds of fucked up shit."

"So you would rather I let clowns disrespect?"

"What about anything that I just said sounded like that?"

He laughed and took a deep breath. "I guess I could calm down some, instead of feeling like I gotta fight the world." He shook his head. "I wonder if most men feel like this or if it's just me."

I shrugged. "I just think you have a lot of pent up hostility." I paused. "And you act it out by fighting."

He leaned back and exhaled. "Listen at you sounding all scholarly."

"I'm serious." I paused. "If you not fighting somebody it's the other thing."

"The other thing being what?" He asked, pumping into me like he wanted to fuck. I could feel him stiffening.

I kissed his lips and then his neck. "The other thing being fucking bitches on the side of the road." I bit down into his neck and he screamed before tossing me off his lap, sending me flying across the floor.

"Ow"! He yelled rubbing the area. "Fuck is wrong with you?" He looked at his hand for blood.

"Nah, what the fuck is wrong with you, my nigga?" I said standing up, rubbing the back of my head, which had bounced on the table. "You think because I'm an addict I'm blind and can't drive and follow your ass—"

"I never said that shit!"

"Then tell me why I pulled up on you getting your dick sucked by some bitch!" I yelled.

I heard heavy footsteps overhead and before long Amina appeared at the top of the steps. "What's going on down there?"

"What's wrong down there?" Russo yelled from upstairs too.

"I got it!" Amina said to Russo before focusing back on us. "What's going on with ya'll?"

Reggie looked at her and then me. "We got it. I'm sorry about the noise."

"That ain't telling me nothing," Amina continued.

"Maybe it's because you ain't supposed to hear nothing," I added.

"Is that right?" She said putting her hands on her hips.

"Look, this situation is between me and mine, Amina," I continued. "Let me tend to mine while you tend to yours."

She nodded, looked at us and walked away.

I sat on the sofa and Reggie sat next to me. I moved a few spaces over, not wanting his whorish body to touch mine anymore. "I'm sorry, Tamika." He paused, reaching out to touch my thigh. I slapped his hand away. "I didn't...I didn't..."

44   BY KIM MEDINA

"Know you would get caught?" I looked at him. "My heart told me I was a lie but I said to myself it can't be so."

He ran his hand down his face. "It's not what you think it is."

"Then what the fuck is it?" I said, tears rolling down my cheek. "I been home less than a week and already you telling me I'm not good enough for you. Already you telling me that I got competition? I thought you were supposed to be there for me. Loving me and supporting me! You promised to be my hero when the whole time you nothing but a villain!"

I moved to get up and he snatched me back to the sofa. Sitting side by side, his arm was around my neck so that I leaned against his right side, almost like he had me in a side headlock. "Don't do this to me, baby." He whispered with heavy breath, the tears from his eyes dampening the top of my hair. "I...I fucked up and—"

"You hurt me. You thought you were slick and you hurt me more than I knew was possible."

"Please forgive me." He begged, his breath quickening. "Without you I'm just another nigga in these streets. I fucking need you."

"Well maybe it needs to be that way." I moved to get up and once again he yanked me back down.

"She won't be a problem unless we let her."

I looked around, my heart thumping wildly. The only thing on my mind in that moment was getting high and I knew if I had access to drugs I would've done just that. It became clear that Reggie was the source of everything good and bad for me and without him I was nothing.

"I don't love her and she could never stand next to you. Let me show you and I promise you won't regret it." He picked me up and put me back on his lap so that I was looking down at him. "Let me show you how much you mean to me." He kissed my lips and I could smell her scent on his body. So why was I turned on? "Let me love you." His dick stiffened and he released himself from his pants, before moving my panties to the side and entering me. "Let, me take care of you." He pumped into me and my head flew back as his dick penetrated my body. "Let me...."

It was a wrap.

Crack wasn't my drug of choice.

Reggie was.

CHAPTER FIVE

REGGIE

Russo had been begging me to grab him a steak and cheese sub and each time I said no, worried about wanting or needing something to take my mind off of my problems. Like some pussy. And just as I thought, the moment I walked outside my dick stiffened with the possibilities of fucking something warm for lunch.

Should I call Tamara to relieve this pressure?

"Nah, you can't do that my nigga." I said to myself. *"You have a wife who already proved she's on her sneaky shit. So what you gotta do is go get this food and head back because no doubt she's clocking you right now."*

After ordering Russo's food from the carryout, I stuffed my hands in my pocket to press down my dick. A nigga been told several times I'm bigger than the average so that's no easy feat. All I wanted to do was get his food and go home before...

Wifey (Text)

Where are you

Me (Text)

Bae I'm getting Russo's food.

Wifey (Text)

Well you taking too long.

Me (Text)

But I literally just pulled up.

Wifey (Text)

Don't make me cut that dick off.

Man, my wife tripping hard now. I'm starting to wonder if it was a bad idea to let her go to rehab. Before she went in she was all sweet and demure but now...now she a whole different bitch. Still sweet but different.

"How you doing?" A Chinese and black hybrid asked walking up to me. She was the perfect amount of light skin and brown that got me going. "You look kinda out of it."

Please, God get this girl away from me before I fuck her. "Nah, I'm good. Just waiting on my brother's food. That's all."

She nodded and moved closer and I could smell the scent of her pussy. Let me clear some things up right here. My scent senses were different than most. But men always claim that a pussy should be odorless and them the same niggas who don't get it on a regular. Every pussy got it's own scent. Some foul and some like the sweet scent of bread but all tell a scent story. And the chick standing next to me was no exception. Her pussy smelled like she'd done some things, but was wise enough to know you couldn't do everybody.

And I wanted a taste.

"So where you going tonight?" She asked, skimming through her social media site like she wasn't catching my every word.

"Chilling."

"Chilling solo or with someone?" She looked at me and blinked her eyes a few times.

I frowned. "What you some kind of hoe or something?" I said. "'Cause I don't pay for the pussy."

Its true.

"Why is it that black brothers and sisters can't have regular conversation? I mean they really put into our minds that any casual talk is something more."

I shrugged. "It ain't my business to talk about economics or sociological types of situations."

She smiled. "A man with big words. I like that."

"Number 456!" The cashier yelled holding up my brown bag wrapped in plastic. "Its ready!"

I moved toward the counter and took my meal before moving to the door. "Wait up," she said.

I stopped even though I shouldn't have. "What for?" I asked sternly, hoping I'd irritate her and she'd move on even though I knew she wouldn't. There was something about my face that told women that it was okay to come on to me, even if they ended up getting this dick a few moments later.

"I really don't have a lot of time." I said.

"Please. It'll only take a few minutes."

She right about that.

Her hands were planted on the roof of the car as if I were the police as I banged her from behind in an alley. She was tight. Not like a virgin, because I had many. But tight enough to let me know she was still selective, despite her whorish tendencies.

"Damn, you feel so good inside of me," she moaned as I continued to pound this dick into her. Raw. As if she were mine. "Just keep it right there. Please."

She didn't have to tell me that. Before long I had splattered into her and afterwards I pulled my clothes up and got into my car without so much as a bye. She let me know how she felt by throwing a black Ugg boot at my ride but what do I care?

I was gone.

Once at home Russo complained loudly at first about how his food was cold until I whispered into his ear what kept me up. Catching the few words I gave him he let it slide, knowing that saying more would cause more problems for my already broken home.

"Where were you?" Tamika asked arms crossed over her chest. "Because something ain't right."

"Nowhere."

Instead of disputing she got mad and stomped upstairs. I was doing all I could to prevent her from getting high but something told me she wanted to use me as an excuse. I could already hear her saying, 'It's because of you I'm smoking again,'. And I wouldn't give her the courtesy.

Walking outside and sitting on the porch, I decided I needed a cigarette, something I didn't do often. Once I lit it and inhaled, I immediately felt relaxed until Tamara stomped up to me with a scowl on her face.

Fuck was she doing around my house?

This bitch is crazy!

CHAPTER SIX

RUSSO

Dinner was perfect tonight.

We sat alone in the living room and listened to PNB Rock as we ate. When I was finished I rubbed my stomach and pushed my wheels on my chair so I was closer to where she sat on the sofa. "That was good, Amina. Thank you. It hit the spot like fuck." I paused. "Listen, I wanted to know if you were able to reach my cousin at my aunt's house?"

She stared at me. "Why? So you can tell him how supposedly mean I am to you?"

"Nah, bae, I just wanted to talk to him that's all. And since his number changed and my aunt ain't got no phone, you gotta go see her in Barry Farms."

"Well like I said I already went over there and she wasn't home." She rolled her eyes.

"Well did you leave the number to my cell then?"

"Yes, Russo." She paused. "Maybe ya'll not as close as you thought."

"I never said close but he always hit me back."
I took a deep breath. "Maybe I'll have Reggie drive
me over there next week." I paused. "Seems odd
you couldn't connect that's all."

She nodded and then opened her mouth like
she wanted to say something that didn't come
out.

"Amina, you can talk to me."

"I know, Russo. That's what I used to love
about you. I could say whatever I need to and you
won't judge. You never do."

I took a deep breath. "I had a dream the other
day. A real good one at that." I touched her leg
and she smiled, something she hadn't done in a
long while.

"Well, are you gonna tell me or do I have to
pinch it out of you?" She said.

I frowned. Was she serious or not? Everything
seemed extra scary in this wheel chair. I had so
many fears that I didn't have to deal with before. I
had fears of being left alone, and forgotten about.
I can't count the number of dreams I had where
everybody I loved died in a car accident, leaving
me in the house alone to starve to death.

Then there were dreams of losing the use of
my arms and even my eyes. I mean I was already

BY KIM MEDINA

confined to a chair, what's to say that my hands and sight wouldn't go next?

So definitely little things that may be said as jokes to other people like her pinching me didn't sit well at all.

"I dreamed that I had my legs under me again and that I took you to the movies, drove you to the house but we didn't go in. Instead we fucked outside like savages." I laughed. "The way we use to."

She smiled. "From the front or back?"

I smirked. "Come on, don't act like you don't like it from the side. With me lifting up that ass cheek so I can get a good peak," I said.

She laughed loud, like it came from her heart and it immediately warmed me.

"I still remember how to touch you, Amina. And how to hold you."

She nodded. "The same but different."

That's what we said all the time so that it wouldn't remind us that I was a nigga who couldn't protect her like I had in the past. Back in the day, when this first happened she told me to pray about being able to move on my own again but lately she didn't say a word about me being on my feet or prayer. She was just mad all the time.

"I love you, Amina."

"You do?"

"With everything I had before and now."

She nodded. "Well tell me a truth I didn't know about you."

I sighed. "I don't know about that shit."

"Why you say that?"

I took a deep breath. "Every time we play that game it ends with you being mad at me. And I don't want that tonight."

She shook her head. "Me either. And yet I would love to hear something from you that comes from somewhere authentic. Something real. Without all this fake romantic shit."

My heartbeat kicked up. Something had gone wrong that quickly. "Fake romantic shit? Everything I'm saying to you is honest. And from the heart."

"So then you wouldn't mind going deeper." She said. "I know something about you, Russo. Something you think I don't know. So I want you to make it easier by being on the one and telling me the truth."

I took a deep breath and scanned my mind on what she could possibly know that would have her so angry with me. I thought about the bitches I might of stabbed sexually *pre* me being married and the one hoe Tamara. As far as I'm concerned everything post should be forgiven because she let the nut nigga Jordan or whatever stab at her. But you gotta understand, my wife is bird crazy. She could be mad at anything.

"Can you give me a clue?"

"Nigga, if you good you shouldn't need a clue. So the fact that you even said that lets me know you still foul."

My heart was thumping harder and I pushed my wheel chair back some to get away from her wrath. "Okay, did I say something to you that you didn't like? Like that time I was talking about taking Naverly? Or that bitch I had up in the crib watching her after I found out about you and old boy?"

She shook her head no and I scratched my head.

"Amina, just tell me, bae. Let's talk about it. You're my wife and if I wronged you I want you to serve it to me right here. Don't...don't do what you been doing by holding it inside."

She frowned. "Do what I been doing?"

"Yeah...the leaving me in the tub and...and kicking me off the bed when I'm vulnerable and shit like that." I paused. "I mean can't you see how wrong that is?"

She stared at me.

Was she listening or not?

Suddenly she got up and I pushed my wheel chair back some more. But she stood over me, locked my chair from moving and got on her knees between my legs. At least she wasn't towering over me like some mad woman and I could feel a little safer.

Next she removed my dick from my pants and diaper which still worked and put me into her mouth. Thank God I hadn't had to use the bathroom yet, so I was clean. I hadn't gotten my boy sucked in I can't even remember how long. And here she was, going down like she needed to do it to pay the bills.

Part of me was nervous that she would chomp down on me at anytime and the other was turned on by the fear. I loved this girl more than I could express and I just wished she knew it.

When she was still sucking after five minutes, I put my hand behind her head and pumped into

BY KIM MEDINA

her mouth harder. I could feel the pressure of my dick about to explode when suddenly she got up right before I unloaded in her mouth.

"Fuck you, nigga."

With wide eyes I shook my head softly from left to right. "Don't do this. Please."

"Suck your own dick, clown," She smiled. "I'm out of here."

"FUCKKKKKKK!!!!!!!" I screamed.

CHAPTER SEVEN

TAMIKA

Reggie was fast asleep as I stared into his closed eyelids. As hard as he was snoring I knew I could do anything to him outside of pain and he wouldn't get up. The thing was he only slept this hard when he fucked and since I knew he wasn't fucking me it made me wonder.

Who had he been with?

Warming up my throat with a soft gurgle, I used all the air I could muscle and spit in his face. My thick yellow phlegm hung off his eyelids and still he remained sleep. I laughed softly as I eased out of bed, took a shower and slipped into something comfortable. My sweat pants and a white t-shirt.

The moment I left our room I saw Russo sitting in the hallway and looking down the steps. Normally Reggie managed to pick him up and place him in his chair after he carried him downstairs but I couldn't.

Instead I sat on the top of the step and looked at him. "I'm not strong enough," I said.

BY KIM MEDINA

"You are," he said softly, not really looking at me.

I smiled. "I mean physically." I looked down. "I can't pick you up to take you downstairs."

He shook his head. "Oh, that's not what I wanted anyway." He sighed and looked at me. "So, how have you been, Tamika?"

I shrugged. "That question can mean a lot of things to a lot of different people."

"I mean how are you since you left rehab?" He continued. "We don't talk much but I do care about you."

I smiled. "I don't know if I like being clean to tell you the truth. Constantly being forced to deal with stuff can be too heavy. I mean, I like the idea of not having to do the grossest things for money but, other than that..."

"I get it."

I looked at him. "Do you really? I mean, niggas like you used to serve me. It was all about the money without caring about who you hurt. So how can you get it?"

"Tamika, I—"

I put my hand up and took a deep breath. "I'm sorry, Russo," I said softly. "But that's what I mean. It's like now that I'm clean my mind is clear and I got all these thoughts that come out at anytime." I placed my hands on the side of my face. "And they keep me in this twisted ball of hate."

"Then you doing right."

"What that mean?"

"It means you should be proud of yourself because at least you're talking about it. You not letting it simmer with no outlet. That's how niggas be going mad."

I nodded and looked at his wheelchair. My mind floated to the time he was helping us fix up this house and how strong he was when he played with Naverly and now, well now things were different.

"How have you been? Since you had to be in this chair and all?"

He shrugged and hit his wheels so that he backed up toward his room. Before entering he turned around and wheeled back toward me. "I need you to do me a favor."

"Short of picking you up or sex, I'm down," I laughed.

"I need you to get in contact with my cousin out New York for me. I haven't heard from him and I wanna talk."

"I ain't got no problem with it."

"Here's the thing, the nigga can't keep the same number and his moms, my auntie, be slacking on the phone bill since I been off the streets and couldn't give her paper. So If you gonna connect for me you gotta go to the house in D.C."

I nodded. "Seems simple enough but how come you didn't ask Amina?"

"Amina has been doing a lot for me. A whole lot, Tamika. I mean, I ain't none of the man I use to be and, well, I think she's getting tired of me. And the last thing I wanna do is burden her with this here."

"When you want me to go?"

"As soon as you can," he said seriously. "Today would be even better."

"Give me the address and I'll see what I can do."

The drive was peaceful on the way to Russo's aunt's house. But the moment I landed in Barry

Farms, I knew anything could happen. People hung outside drinking liquor openly and everybody with a set of eyes kept them on me as I parked in front of his aunt's place.

After knocking on the door to the address he gave me I was about to run back in my car when someone yelled, "Who the fuck is it?"

"Uh...I...uh..."

The door flew open and a big woman with a mustache and beard answered. She wore a long yellow muumuu and her titties swung outward like front wings. "Who the fuck is you?" She placed her hands on her hips.

"I'm a friend of Russo's."

Her eyes widened as she pushed open the screen door causing it to squeak and slam behind her. She stepped outside in front of me and the stale smell of living in there forever hit me in the face. "Russo...how is he?"

"He fine, considering he got shot and is in a wheel chair and all." I said.

She took a deep breath. "Yeah, I heard. Sad about it for real."

A large pop sounded off behind me and she noticed my nervousness. "I guess you not use to all this are you?"

"I'm from D.C. but definitely not this part."

She sighed. "Well none of us gonna be around here much longer anyway. They redeveloping the area from projects into homes." She shook her head. "And I have no idea where we gonna go after that shit happens."

I nodded. "Well Russo wanted me to give Cambridge his number." I looked behind her toward the house. "Is he here?"

"Chile, Cambridge is gonna be Cambridge. Living in New York he comes to check on me sometimes and other times not so much. But if you leave your info I'll be sure to tell him."

I gave her the closed handwritten note Russo gave me and turned to leave.

"And if you ever want me to suck on that little pussy of yours, because I'm sure it's cute, come on over here anytime. You hear me?"

I frowned and took off running to my car.

CHAPTER EIGHT

TAMIKA

When I walked toward my house a pretty girl approached me from behind. "Excuse me, but can I talk to you for a minute?"

I looked around and pointed at myself. "Me?"

She nodded and looked nervously around. "Yes. But I would prefer if we could go somewhere and get some drinks. My treat." She grinned again, fingering her long black hair.

"What is this about?"

She took a deep breath. "Russo."

Twenty-five minutes later we were in Fridays at the bar. I was having coffee with extra sugar since I couldn't drink and she was on her second martini and I still didn't know what she wanted with my sister's husband. It was dumb to even follow her here but what could be the harm?

Plus I needed the adventure.

"So are you gonna tell me what you want with Russo or not?" I asked.

"How is he?"

I shrugged. It was the second time I had been forced to answer that question for the day. "He's

66   BY KIM MEDINA

in a wheelchair. I think you can guess how the rest goes."

She nodded. "I use to date him."

"I figured as much." I paused. "But you do know he's married and with my sister now don't you?"

She took a deep breath. "Yeah, and for some reason it took me long to understand why he picked her over me."

"Fuck is that supposed to mean?" I asked.

She extended her hand. "I'm sorry. I definitely didn't mean it that way. I mean, if you knew Russo as long as I did then you'd get it. I'm saying, Russo's a trap nigga and trap niggas don't usually settle down with quiet girls. I guess she must've been the one if they still together."

"Yes, they still together and they not planning on being apart any time soon."

"And I wouldn't want them to." She said with a little attitude. I guess she was tired of being fake nice. "Plus I saw their daughter and she looks just like both of them."

"Hold up, when you see her?" I frowned.

"The day Russo was shot at." She paused. "She was playing in the balls with the other kids and then came out. And I saw Amina at the restaurant before that, when Russo was going to New York." She looked down. "It just seems so sad that he's caught up like that right now, in that chair. They said they didn't even find the man who did it. Ain't that something?"

My breathing increased but I didn't know why. "How you know where we lived anyway?"

"I knew that house before ya'll lived there." She said. "A bunch of dealers used to move work out of that spot and some bad things happened to Russo there too. Ask him about it, he'll tell you."

My eyebrows rose. "Like what?"

"I won't say too much. I will say he was raped."

I put my hand over my chest. "What...I...I...ain't nobody tell me nothing like...like that."

"Why would he?" She shrugged. "He was ashamed." She shook her head. "Girls being taken advantage of is bad but when it happens to boys the scars are forever."

I didn't believe her.

"What did you...what did you say your name was again?"

"I didn't."

She's right. In my quest to feel something outside of getting high I followed this chick to a restaurant where anybody could be waiting around to hurt me. What was I thinking? If I could even call it that.

"Well what is your name?"

She smiled slyly. It was wide and long as if she knew something I didn't and was loving it. "Tamara."

"Well, Tamara, I'm warning you to stay the fuck away from Russo." I said, pointing at her.

"Well that ain't gonna be a problem. You see, I'm not after Russo no more. That nigga can't do shit for me but roll up out my face. But that Reggie," she grinned and licked her lips. "Now that Reggie is kinda sweet."

I stood up. "Fuck does this have to do with my husband?"

"Let's just say when I lap up his cum, I love the way he smells. It's always so sweet. I wonder if it's you."

I pulled back my hand and slapped her in the face. She absorbed it and laughed like it didn't hurt. "If I see you again it's gonna be on."

"On like it was when I popped up to the house the other day and Reggie snuck me around back and fucked me in the house he used to stay in? Because if you talking about that kind of on I may be willing to play."

"You a lying bitch."

"If you really believed that why you crying?"

"I...I want you to stay the fuck away from me!" I ran out toward my car.

TAMIKA

Sitting in my car, a fifty-dollar bill clutched in my hand I tried to give myself a good reason not to go around the way and buy some drugs. Reggie said he would do right by me and now I'm finding out *again* that it's all a lie. If he don't care enough to hold me down then why am I even here? What's the use of living?

I was just about to pull off to find some drugs when my phone rang. I wasn't going to answer it at first but something deep in my spirit told me to. Removing the phone from my purse I took a deep breath, wiped the tears off my face and answered.

BY KIM MEDINA

"Tamika." A man said.

"Who...who is this?" I wiped my tears away again.

"It's Murphy, your sponsor. For some reason you were on my heart. How you doing?"

I broke down in tears.

CHAPTER NINE

AMINA

Sitting in Naverly's room helping her do her homework, at some point I started daydreaming when she grabbed my face, her breath smelling like apple candy. "Are you gonna help me finish, mommy?"

I blinked a few times. "Yes, baby girl. I'm sorry I...I wasn't paying you much attention."

"Are you okay, mommy?"

"Yes. But listen, how 'bout you finish your homework and I go check on daddy. Okay?"

She nodded and left. When I walked into our room Russo was laying on the bed, his hand on his belly the other behind his head. He looked like he use to before I found out he was a liar and he got shot. When shit between us was regular and sweet.

"Everything okay?" He asked turning his focus from the game and onto me.

"Yeah, everything's cool. I thought I heard you call me." I lied.

"Nah. I'm just watching TV."

I sat on the bed and looked at the television although I didn't know what was going on or cared. "Who's winning?"

"The Cowboys." He said. "The game came on yesterday but I didn't have a chance to watch it. Doing it now."

I nodded. "Listen, I'm sorry about how things have been going on between us."

"Amina, for real, I don't wanna talk right now."

My eyebrows rose. "And why is that?"

"Because every time we talk we go into this weird place that makes things worse than when we started. For real all I want to do is mind my business and stay out your way."

"So what about cleaning up behind you?"

"I got some things in motion."

"Like what?"

"I had Tamika reach out to my cousin." He said. "When he hit me back then I'll have one of my girl cousins stop by and check on me from time to time. That way you can—"

I stood up and slapped him. "You ungrateful ass nigga!"

"What are you talking about?" He yelled, lifting up on his elbows.

"You gonna bring somebody else up in my house without even telling me? Are you crazy or something?"

"You're the one who's fucking crazy! One minute you say you tired of me and the next you act like you trying to keep me from my family."

"Nigga, ain't nobody trying to keep you from your dry ass family? You just—"

"Then why ain't my aunt reach out?" He yelled. "Huh?" She may have shit with her but when it comes to me she don't play."

"So you saying I'm lying about—"

BEEP. BEEP. BEEP.

I rushed over to the window and saw a truck out front I didn't recognize. It was a black pick up truck with gold rims.

BEEP! BEEP! BEEP!

Russo sat up straight. "Who's that?" He asked. "Is that my cousin?"

"Don't worry about all that." I told him. "We'll finish this conversation later."

I smoothed my hair with my fingers and ran out before bolting down the stairs and out the front door. Once there I was standing in front of Cambridge, Russo's cousin from New York.

"Hey, pretty lady," he said looking me over. "Although it looks like you've been through some things and ain't keeping it tight like you used to. But how you doing?"

I crossed my arms over my chest. "What are you doing here?"

"Well since you and I haven't started our love affair yet," he said touching my waist before putting his hands into his pocket. "I must be here for my cousin." He looked behind me. "Where is he?"

"He ain't here."

He frowned. "That don't make a lot of sense."

"And why is that?"

"For starters he in a wheel chair. Now I don't know about what you think but to me that would make it hard for him to get around." He paused. "So you wanna start again?"

"Hold up. You saying I'm lying?"

"Would never think of it."

"Because it sounds like that."

He nodded. "Okay," He grew serious. "My cousin ain't never say nothing but good things about you and I don't see why now would change." He paused. "So how 'bout this." He rubbed his hands together. "You tell me where my family is and I'll pop up on him right quick. To surprise him. And show him I still fuck with the little nigga and shit."

"Like I said, I don't know where he is." I cleared my throat.

"Wow. So you *really* gonna play it like that?"

"I'm his wife not his keeper."

"I get all that. But now I'm gonna have to call you out to be a liar." He pointed at me. "'Cause there ain't no way on this side of Baltimore that a man rolling around in a wheel chair wouldn't tell his wife were he be at." He paused. "So again...where is he?"

I frowned. "You do know Russo's broke right?"

He smiled. "And you telling me that because..."

"When have you ever come into the picture except when you wanted money? Huh? Name one time when you visited this house or his other without asking for a handout."

"That's not true."

"That's all true. Now if you don't get up out my face there's gonna be a problem." I walked into the house and slammed the door behind myself.

CHAPTER TEN
TAMIKA

"So I been trying to keep focused and sometimes things throw me for a loop but then, then I try to remember the places I was in and the things I had to do to stay this way you know?" I said to Murphy. He was sitting next to me on the sofa in our house. "I just wanna be clean. And not give up on all my work."

If you saw him on the street you'd never know he was a prior heroin addict. Standing over six feet tall with skin like yellow caramel he looked good enough to eat. Even the small dreads he kept his hair in were neat and he looked like a well put together rap star instead of my sponsor. What's best is that when he looks into my eyes, it's as if he's looking through me.

"One day at a time, Cherry. That's all you can do." He called me Cherry because when I was in rehab I used to eat them by the jars. Something about the taste and feel of the skin on my tongue made me feel alive and sexual.

I took a deep breath. "I'm trying."

He looked at me closer and put a hand on my thigh. "What else is it?" He removed his hand. "You can talk to me. I mean you are definitely beautiful but I'm not here to look at you. I'm here as a crutch. Lean on me."

I took a deep breath. "I think my husband is being unfaithful." I paused. "I mean, he *is* being unfaithful."

"Wow."

"And when I think about it as hard as I've been it makes me want to use again."

He nodded. "I understand, Tamika. I truly do. But people will always act and do things that don't fit into our plan for our lives. And if you base your drug free lifestyle on others it's a recipe for disaster."

"But you don't get it."

"Then help me get it." He paused. "Explain to me how you would go through all those months of rehab only to give it up when your husband fails you?"

"It's not that easy."

"Of course not. It's the hardest thing ever but it's the truth." He moved closer and I could smell the scent of soap on his skin. "Do you know why I wanted to be your sponsor?"

I shook my head no.

"Because I see myself in you."

I smiled. "Well I certainly don't know how I feel about you saying I look like a man."

"Not even close." He said. "I'm talking about having the strength inside to move mountains but feeling like you always need some help." He paused. "You have the power to do all things but you have to accept or reject the people in your life just the way they are."

"What does that mean?"

"It means this." He took a deep breath. "Let's assume your husband is cheating."

"He is. I caught him. Well, I saw him with some girl but I didn't see her face."

"That's even better." He paused. "Let's say you saw him with your own eyes, which you have. Now what?"

"He said he was going to stop."

"But what if he doesn't?" He paused. "You are at the point where you're gonna have to accept that the man who pledged his life to you will never change or leave."

I shook my head. "But I don't know how to be alone."

"You don't have to be alone. You have me." He touched me again and my body trembled.

"You're saying that now but the other night I called your girlfriend answered the phone and—"

"Negative." He said with a smile.

"So it was a man?"

"Double negative." He paused. "I don't have a girlfriend I have friends."

I nodded. "So you're single?"

He took a deep breath. "I'm gonna be honest since that's what we do. I have over ten years of a drug free lifestyle but the ego in me found another thing to latch itself to."

"And what's that?"

"Women."

I was disappointed. "Wow. So you traded one drug for another?"

"Yes and no." He paused. "For starters I don't have anyone in my life I've made a commitment to." He paused. "That means I have a little time to get myself together. And secondly the young lady who answered my home phone when you called is actually someone I had to say goodbye to."

I exhaled. "Now you're scaring me. The last thing I want to do is drop one habit for another one."

"Exactly. Which is why I'm telling you to give up on your husband so you can really be clean. He doesn't deserve—"

"Who the fuck are you?" Reggie said to Murphy before tossing his keys on the table and stomping toward us.

I stood up and moved toward him. "Reggie, this is Murphy. My sponsor I was telling you about."

"Well he look like a nigga hitting on my wife to me," he said through clenched teeth.

"Brother, if I wanted your—"

"I ain't your fucking brother!" Reggie yelled. "Get the fuck up out my house before I lay hands on you."

Murphy nodded politely and turned to me. "I'll be here if you need me."

Suddenly Reggie stole him in the face, causing blood to gush from Murphy's mouth and splash onto my eyelids.

"REGGIE NO!" I yelled holding my face. "WHY?"

"It's okay," Murphy said holding his lips. "But remember what I said. Because this is your future if you stay with this nigga." Murphy walked passed Reggie and out the door.

When he was gone Reggie moved toward me and grabbed my hand. "NIGGA, FUCK YOU!" I yelled before snatching my hand away and taking off up the steps.

CHAPTER ELEVEN

REGGIE

Man, my wife had my head twisted. Even though I didn't act the most responsible what did she expect when she brought that nigga up in here?

Craziness.

It wasn't until later on that night that I found out Tamara stepped to her in front of the house. I don't care what I do, or how horny I get, I'm done with that bitch. The girl too dangerous and Russo tried to let me know from the onset and I didn't listen.

I was sitting on the step, on my third beer, when Cambridge's truck pulled up. On the real I didn't feel for that nigga. But he was Russo's people and I had to roll with it. So I gulped the rest of my beer walked over to him and shook his hand. "What up?"

"Man, is my cousin up in there or not?" He asked.

"Yeah, but why you moving like that? Like you gotta an attitude."

"Because I came by the other day to check on him and his wife gonna say he wasn't in the crib."

I scratched my head and tried to think of a day where Russo wasn't here. I stopped when I was unsuccessful. "I don't know 'bout all that but he definitely home now. Come on in."

Ten minutes later I got Russo dressed, put on his freshest gear and carried him downstairs. Afterwards he was saying shit I didn't believe. I mean if he was right the wildest things were going on right up under my nose. "I know it's hard to believe," he continued. "But I think if I stay here my wife is gonna kill me."

"Russo, man, if this was going on why didn't you tell me? You did say something about turning the water cold and all that but you really think she would kill you?" I asked. "No way I would've allowed it to move like this."

"I didn't want to get you involved." He removed his cap, scratched his head and put it back on.

"So you let her hit you and not feed you and shit like that?" I asked. "Then you have my wife go get your cousin instead of telling me first."

"To be honest, I didn't trust you," Russo said.

I took one step back. "And why is that?" I crossed my arms over my chest.

"Because I know you fucking old girl."

I was gut punched. "Tamara?"

"Who you think?" Russo asked, his nose flaring.

"Wow, what ya'll got going on up in this bitch," Cambridge laughed clapping his hands like he was watching a show. "The wife on some Misery shit and my mans over here smashing your number two. What's coming of this world if you can't trust the niggas in your circle?"

"I don't know," I said looking at him. "How 'bout you tell me."

Cambridge pointed at himself. "Hold up, this my fault?"

"All I'ma say is this," I started. "My man been shot up for a minute. But it took my old lady to knock on your door to get you to come over here to see about him? How foul is that?"

"Because I thought the nigga was locked up."

"Why you thought that?" Russo asked him.

"Everybody know you got that pending case, man." He shrugged. "Anyway I'm here now. So what you wanna do?"

Russo took a deep breath. "You got a place to stash me until I figure some shit out?"

"Yeah, but you think you gonna last long enough until I get it together?" Cambridge paused. "Because I'm living in an apartment in Brooklyn but my mans just bought a house. It's gonna take a second to get it squared away though but you'll have more room there."

"Yeah I think I can wait." Russo folding his arms over his chest.

"No doubt, no doubt," Cambridge said scratching his head. "You got some bread though? 'Cause my man is cool but he ain't in the charity type of mood if you catch my drift."

Russo took a deep breath. "I can scratch up a little something."

"Good, good," Cambridge said rubbing his hands again. "So hold fast on anything else. I'ma talk to him and I'll be through in a couple of days."

"Man, don't leave me stranded," Russo said.

"I won't but you should be good here for a little while," Cambridge laughed. "Your mans over here sounding like he on that rescue shit so it should be smooth sailing." Cambridge shook Russo's hand and walked out.

When we were alone I wheeled him into the living room and sat on the sofa. "How you find out about Tamara?"

"She told me."

I shook my head. "That bird is scandalous!"

"Exactly, which is why I don't understand how you could get with her."

"Man, I think something wrong with me." I said rubbing my head. "Its like, when shit be going crazy all I wanna do is smash something. And she ran into me one day after you got shot and 'Mika was in that rehab spot and...and..."

"You let her suck your dick," Russo said.

"Basically," I replied, both of us laughing. "For me it's like problems and sex go hand and hand and I be trying to stop it but I can't. It's like it takes over me."

"Are you safe?" Russo asked.

I frowned. "How you sound?"

"You wearing condoms or not?"

"Sometimes, but I be knowing when they clean and shit." I told him. "Trust me I'm good."

He shook his head. "Whatever, man. It's your dick. But I will say this, that chick ain't nothing but trouble. That's why the pussy so good because she stay crazy and crazy bitches always got the tightest, best shit. But she will fuck up everything you love if you keep her around. That's on everything."

I nodded. "I know."

"In the meantime keep a look out for me. I didn't wanna get you involved because of Tamika but I don't know what's going on with Amina. It's like she's mad at me for something and instead of telling me what's on her mind she trying to drag it out. I don't know her anymore."

"I got you, man. I'll be looking out for real. Believe that."

CHAPTER TWELVE

AMINA

I helped Russo into the tub like I always did and turned the water off once he was inside. He was quiet since yesterday, barely asking me for anything or saying more than thank you or no thank you. Reggie brought his food and spent most of his time with him, leaving me to have to change him or bathe him only once a day.

"Russo, what's going on?"

He shook his head and wiped himself with the soapy red washcloth. "Nothing, bae. Why you keep asking me that?"

I shrugged. "I don't know. Something feels off."

He shrugged too. "I think you looking into things deeper than need be."

"But you don't ask me for anything. Reggie spent all day with you yesterday and today too. So what's up for real?"

He took a deep breath. "Amina, I'm confused. You act like doing things for me is the worst thing in the world. And when I push back on asking for help it's a problem? Not to mention you holding me back from seeing my people. It's like you turned crazy or something."

I took a deep breath. "You exaggerating now. Things ain't been the best but still…"

"Well that's how I feel and that's why I didn't wanna talk."

"So I'm the villain huh?"

"Never said that."

"But you were thinking it." He shook his head and remained silent. So I grabbed his feet and pulled, forcing his back to fall flat in the tub and the water to cover his face. "How you feel now huh?" I yelled. "How you feel now!" He struggled to get up using his arms, but was no match for my angered strength.

Suddenly the door flew open and Reggie pushed me to the side before rushing to the tub to help Russo out. "Fuck is wrong with you?" Reggie yelled at me. "Huh?" He held Russo's wet body in his arms.

I backed up, looking down at my hands. As the months went by I became resentful and even hateful. I didn't even recognize myself in the mirror. And now, now I was sure that if Reggie hadn't come in when he did I would've killed my husband.

Ashamed, I backed out and ran away.

AMINA

I sat in a chair in Tamika's room and watched her sleep. Reggie had taken Russo outside to get some air and I just wanted silence. And I found it by watching my sister sleep peacefully.

When her cell phone rang I picked it up and answered and saw a text message that gave me chills.

DRILLO

U forgot bout me? I thought we were goin down 2gether. U and me against the world.

Her phone trembled in my hand and I felt my pressure rising. It's like he was dead set on bringing her to hell like he had done to himself. I hit him from her phone.

ME

Meet me by Reggies house.

I knew from talks with Tamika that they spent some time there and figured it would be as good a place as any to confront my brother. And fifteen minutes later I caught him sneaking up to the house.

"Drillo!" I yelled. He was about to run when he saw me instead of her but I said, "You hear me out and I got some money for you."

When he moved closer I wanted to cry. His white t-shirt was almost black and his blue jeans looked brown. "What you want with me? And why you fake like you Tamika on text?"

"Why you doing this, Drillo? This ain't right."

"Doing what?"

"It's like you the devil or something. Trying to take her down with you." I moved closer. "I mean, I thought you said you were going to get clean? I thought you said you were gonna let her go."

"I never told you that." He crossed his arms over his chest.

"You did."

He took a deep breath. "Well people say a lot of shit they don't mean when they want a little high." He paused. "But look, you said you got some money so where its at? I might as well get what I came for since I'm here."

"I'm not giving you nothing."

"Then I'll stand outside of the house everyday until she sees me. Because I know what to say to get her to have one more taste. I know the points to remind her of. I know what she's afraid of and what she loves."

He smiled, before moving his hips. I could tell right away that it took the drugs for him to embrace who he really was, a gay man.

"Even if she don't get high at first what you think my presence will remind her of, Amina?" He continued. "Huh? The good times. The carefree times when we used to get high until the sun came up."

"I can't believe what I'm hearing, Drillo. Please tell me why you doing this?"

"Because ya'll bitches abandoned me! Because ya'll acted like I was the problem when for real it was what happened to me."

"And I get that. Wesley using you for sex was wrong. But how much longer are you gonna blame everybody else?"

"I don't know, how 'bout you tell me?"

"Excuse me."

"Look at yourself." He said. "Your hair all over your head. Your clothes is regular and you got bags under your eyes. Looks like to me that before you start pointing a finger this way you better look in the mirror at yourself." He put his hands out. "Now are you gonna give me the money or do I really gotta perform?"

"I should've let Russo kill you." The moment I said the words I wished I could take them back because they were not true.

"Then maybe you'll be smarter next time because for real, I don't give a fuck anymore." A single tear trailed down his face.

I reached in my pocket and handed him ten bucks. "It's all I got."

He rolled his eyes. "Don't worry, missy, It'll do for now."

He switched away and I broke down crying.

CHAPTER THIRTEEN
RUSSO

It had been three days and I still didn't hear from my cousin. To make shit worse, Reggie had been out of the house looking around for Tamika who was sleeping wherever. And since Amina was left alone with me, she made it her life's duty to continue to make my life hell.

Again.

I gotta get out of here but I don't know how. I even asked Amina to let me sleep downstairs on the sofa, that way I could roll myself out the door but she vetoed that shit quick. Her plan was to keep me helpless and under her thumb and I hated her for it.

I rolled to my cell phone and tried to think of someone to dial. Suddenly the weirdest person came to mind but I shrugged it off and said fuck it, let me shoot my shot.

The phone rang once before she answered. "What you want, Russo?"

"How you been?" I said smiling, hoping she would think I really gave a fuck.

"What do you want, boy?" She said louder.

I took a deep breath. "Tamara, look, I know you fucked up with me."

"Do you really?"

"Yes. I mean, I shot you in the hand and then I pushed you out my car. But please understand, life ain't been real good for me either. I definitely got paid back and then some."

She laughed.

I frowned. "Fuck is so funny?"

"I'm trying to understand why you think I should give a fuck about any of this."

I took a deep breath. "Because you said you loved me right? You said you wanted to be with me back in the day. So if that's true now is your chance."

"Let me get this straight. So now that you got wheels for feet I'm supposed to—"

"You know what, bitch!"

She laughed harder. "There we go. Now I'm hearing the true Russo come to light." She giggled again. "Listen, I'm gonna save you from having to spread your lips any further. Don't ask me shit because I'm not doing anything for you. Besides, I'm with Reggie now."

I scratched my head. "You mean right now?"

"No, stupid. I'm talking about a relationship."

My eyebrows rose. "You sure 'bout that? Because the man seems to be serious about his wife."

"He is, for now." She giggled. "But just like you hitting me for this pussy, he'll do the same the moment that dry bitch gets him wrong. All I gotta do is buy time and wait."

"Fuck you!"

"No, fuck you!"

I hung up on her and wheeled myself to the top of the steps again. I had one idea left that I didn't want to put into motion unless I had to. And now, after not seeing anybody for a day and a half I think now is the time. So I backed up as far as I could go and wheeled myself down the stairs.

TAMIKA

I called Murphy three times since he left my house and nothing. My fear was that if I didn't talk to him in the next couple of minutes, I would do something that I would regret later. The urge was so strong that it was driving me crazy and it felt like every part of my body itched with cravings.

"God, please help me," I said to myself. "I don't know what I'm gonna do."

To make shit crazier, I hadn't spoken to Drillo in three days. I must've accidently deleted his phone number out of my cell because when I searched for it I couldn't find it and now I was waiting on him to call. The fact that I couldn't get through to him is a good thing. Maybe it's God's way of giving me some time to get over this hump.

I was walking down the street trying to figure out what I was going to do when Reggie pulled up on me. I looked at him, rolled my eyes and tried to go the other way.

"Tamika, get in here!" He yelled, following me slowly. "I need to talk to you."

"What you want?" I said as I continued to walk.

"Listen, I'm at a point right now where I don't know myself. Please don't make me get out this car and prove it to you." He paused. "Get over here. Now!"

I stopped walking, took a deep breath and stomped toward the car. No I didn't want to see him after what he did to Murphy. And no I didn't want to talk. But Reggie had been proving to me that he's part crazy so I didn't want my ass whipped either.

I eased in, slammed the door and said, "What?"

He yanked my hair and pulled me toward him. "Where the fuck you been? Huh?"

"Get off me!" I yelled slapping him in the eyes.

He let me go. "Why you haven't been in the house? Huh? Fuck is wrong with you?"

I rubbed my throbbing scalp. "What do you want, Reggie? Because I don't have time for this shit."

"I asked you a question."

I looked out ahead and tried to calm down by taking several deep breaths. "What you did the other day to my sponsor was wrong. And because of you I can't get in touch with him anymore."

"So it's my fault that nigga ignoring you?"

"Yes!" I yelled. "Contrary to what you may believe he wasn't some dude trying to smash. He was helping me stay clean and now he's missing in action."

"Man, fuck that nigga," he said waving the air.

"You see what I'm saying?" I paused. "You didn't used to be like this."

"And you didn't used to be like this either." He said looking into my eyes. "Yeah it's fucked up that I smashed old boy's lip. And I been thinking about it ever since. But whether you believe me or not he wants you."

"No he don't, Reggie."

"I was in the house for only five minutes and I could see how old boy was staring at you. It was all in his eyes."

"Reggie, in your mind everybody wanna fuck because you wanna fuck everybody." I pointed in his face. "All this is, is your guilt!"

He scratched his head. "That ain't true."

"Do you realize how ridiculous this conversation is? Huh? All of two days ago I caught you in the car letting some slut suck your dick and because you out in these streets you try to flip the script on me now?"

His breath increased. "You can't be out here like this, Tamika. I'm not gonna stand for it."

"What does that mean?"

"Exactly what I said." He paused. "You an addict but you also my wife. And wives are supposed to obey their husbands. I think you need to remember our—"

I threw his car in drive, opened my door and ran out. "TAMIKA!" I heard him yelling as he just stopped his car from hitting the one in front of it by turning the wheel. "COME BACK!"

Reggie could scream all he wanted. I was gone.

CHAPTER FOURTEEN

REGGIE

I was parked behind the McDonald's while jerking my dick. It was hard at first to get one off until I saw this slut with tight jeans and her ass hanging out walk by. Once at her car she bent down in her driver's seat like she was looking for something. From my view I could see her pussy open up like a peach split into two because I could tell she wasn't wearing panties.

Slut.

After getting my shit off I wiped my hand with some napkins in my car and tossed them out the window.

"Fuck! What am I gonna do about my wife? And what am I going to do with myself?"

It's like things were going good and then, well, then shit went to the left. I tried to be everything their mother wanted me to be at first, I really did. But before they came into the picture all I had to be concerned about was myself. Now I got a wife and three people more dysfunctional than me. How am I supposed to survive?

When my phone rang I answered. "Hello."

BY KIM MEDINA

"Hey, sexy," Tamara said.

"Bitch, what you want?" I asked pulling into traffic. "Because I swear to God when I see you I'ma lay hands."

"So you still mad about that?"

"Why would you step to my wife in the first place? Huh? It wasn't like it was gonna change anything in our marriage."

She laughed. "As crazy as she was acting please don't pretend like it didn't cause problems."

"So you did do that shit to ruin my life?" I asked her, my nostrils flaring.

"Never said that." She continued. "Just said that I knew she was crazy and probably went off on you that's all."

"You know what, bitch, suck a dick." I hung up and tossed the phone in the passenger seat.

Fifteen minutes later I was in front of our house parked and trying to get my mind clear before going inside. What were we missing all of a sudden? Shit was so sweet in the house with my fam in the beginning. What had gone wrong? I always believed this house was cursed but now I'm really starting to thing that it's true. Maybe I should burn it down good this time. Be done with it once and for all.

After parking my car and getting out I walked up to the door and opened it. When I was inside I saw Russo lying on the floor at the foot of the steps.

"What the fuck?" I yelled. "What happened?"

"Call 911!" He screamed. "I think I broke my arm!"

AMINA

I was sitting in my cousin April's apartment a few blocks down from my house. She was doing real good for herself too. At first, when things initially went down after Russo got shot she was living with us and helping me take care of Naverly. But now Naverly spent more time over here than she did at my house.

"Thanks for watching her again," I said as I sipped on some Moscato she gave me.

"I wish you stop saying that," She said sitting next to me. "That little girl got my blood so she good." I took a deep breath, then a sip and busted out crying. She placed her hand on my shoulder. "Amina, what's wrong? Oh my God, please don't cry." She rubbed my shoulder softly. "Talk to me."

"I think I'm going...I think I'm going crazy."

"But why do you think that?"

I wiped the tears from my face and shook my head softly from left to right. "April, I...I am so miserable." I stopped moving my head and placed my wine glass on the table. "Everyday I get up and...and I wanna stay in bed. And I hate myself for it."

"Did something happen recently?" She looked behind her at her bedroom door to make sure Naverly didn't hear us. Luckily she was still sleep on the bed.

"It's just a build up." I said.

"Well what have you been doing differently?"

At first I was about to say anything until I thought long and hard about what she meant. It took some time but after awhile I knew exactly what stopped in my life. In the past I used to ask my mother to watch over my family and me. To make sure my daughter was safe from harm. But now, well now I was too angry to talk to her or God.

Yes it all originally started with my husband. Russo lied about the reason he was shot. He lied about somebody breaking into the house too and he'd put his hands on me a lot before he got put in a wheelchair. But what I should've did was leave the marriage and take my daughter, not treat him like I'd done.

"I...I haven't been praying." I wiped my tears away. "Russo hurt me so bad that...I let the anger consume me and now...I don't wanna be nice. I wanna be mad and make him feel like I do."

She placed her hand on my leg. "You are allowed to be mad, cousin. You really are. Now you just have to put your life back together little by little." She sighed. "Listen, my place is not big but you are welcome to have my bedroom. I'll sleep on the couch and with my job at Giant grocery store I can pay our bills. For a little while anyway."

I looked at her and my heart opened up so much. "How were you, how were you able to turn your life around, April? I mean, at one moment you were living with your father in that nasty apartment, fucking my boyfriend behind my back, becoming homeless and even living with me. But now..."

She giggled. "Girl, yes. I definitely did the most." She shook her head. "And when I tell my boyfriend about those days he don't even believe me." She took a deep breath. "But I made it because you were there. When you have someone who sincerely loves you, Amina, I'm telling you." She smiled with a peace I wanted for myself. "There's nothing like it." She pulled me into a hug. "And I'm gonna do the same for you."

I cried in her arms.

When I separated from her I wiped my tears again. "But first, we have got to get your hair done, go to the house and grab you some clothes and give you a fresh start," she continued.

"But what about Russo?" I took a deep breath. "I can't leave him alone."

"God is gonna take care of all of that, trust me. I'm gonna take care of you though. Besides, if you biting him and pinching his face the last thing you need to do is be around him right now."

I laughed. "I never said I pinched his face."

She laughed harder. "You know what I mean." She paused. "Trust me, it will all work out."

I don't know why but in that moment I really believed her.

BY KIM MEDINA

CHAPTER FIFTEEN

TAMIKA

Drillo and me were sitting in Reggie's old house looking at the walls. We were able to gather $40.00 for some drugs, only for them to be fake. And now broke and confused, I didn't know what to do next.

"You think this happened to me on purpose?" I asked Drillo who was scratching his arms and neck.

"Man, what we gonna do now?" He said ignoring my question. "Did you even think to ask Reggie?"

I leaned my head toward him. "Ask Reggie what? For some money for drugs? Are you insane?"

"Basically."

"Drillo, didn't I just tell you that he almost went off on me earlier today?" I paused. "If he even knew I was smoking he'd probably, man, I don't even wanna think about it. I'm just—"

When my cell phone rang I answered. Looking down at the screen I was happy to see it was from my sponsor. If ever there was a time for him to call me now was it. I stood up and walked toward the living room, kicking some trash Drillo and me accumulated from sneaking in here over time out of my way. "Murphy," I said softly.

"Hey, Cherry," he said sounding different than he had in the past. It was like he was talking through his teeth. "How you?"

"I been looking for you. Calling your phone and stuff like that. Why didn't you hit me back?"

"You want the long story or the short one?"

"Any story at this point."

All of a sudden I smelled a bad odor and when I turned around my brother was staring at me. "Who is that?" Drillo whispered walking up behind me.

I covered the phone with my hand. "None of your business," I whispered, walking further away.

"Your man broke my jaw," Murphy continued.

My eyes widened. "Oh my God, Murphy, I'm so sorry. You must hate me right now."

"Actually I don't." He paused. "As a matter of fact I'm out in front of your house. Where are you now?"

My heart rate kicked up. "Murphy, please get away from there. Meet me down the street. On the corner. I promise I'm coming now."

"Hurry up, Tamika. I'm waiting."

I ended the call and walked toward the door.

"Who was that?" Drillo asked.

"It's a friend of mine." I said holding my nose. "And I might be able to work some stuff out to get us good. In the meantime please go get some clean clothes."

"From where?"

"Anywhere. You smell like shit."

"Oh yeah," he said looking down. "My bowels released a little." He paused. "It happens sometimes. But hurry up back."

I shook my head, left the house and walked to the corner. Murphy was in an older model white Yukon and I got in and smoothed my messy ponytail with my hand as if it didn't need a brush. I eased into his truck.

"What you doing out here?" I looked around to see if Reggie was coming.

He looked ahead and then back at me. "To be honest, I had plans to lay hands on your man."

When I looked into his mouth I saw a plastic material binding his teeth. "Please don't do that."

"I'm not." He took a deep breath. "But it did have me wondering about you. And if you were safe or not."

I looked ahead. "I'm fine."

"You don't look like it. As a matter of fact it look like you ain't been getting much sleep. What's good with you? For real."

"Life, Murphy."

He shook his head. "You coming with me." He turned his truck on and pulled away.

"But I can't."

"Don't tell me what you can't do." He paused. "You out here, five seconds from getting high again and expect me to leave?" He paused. "Oh trust me, I can tell the creep up when I see it. Had I not rolled up on you when I did it would've been over."

"Murphy."

He slowed down and parked. "Tell me I'm lying right now and I'll let you go."

I looked to my left. "Exactly." When he pulled off again we rolled passed Drillo who looked at the truck, confused. "Who was that dusty nigga?"

I sat back and put my seatbelt on. "Nobody."

CHAPTER SIXTEEN

AMINA

When I walked into the hospital room Russo was looking at television. I stood next to his bed and his eyes laid on me for one second before falling off of me.

"I'm so sorry, Russo."

He smirked. "Is that right?"

"Of course I am," I said softly. "I would never want you to be in a predicament like that."

"Is that why you left me in the house alone overnight?" He paused before looking back at the television. "It don't even matter. Please, get the fuck up out my face."

"Russo, can you cut the TV off?"

"No."

"Russo, please!"

He took a deep breath, turned off the television and looked at me. "What you want, Amina? Because right now all I want is to be left alone. I don't feel good anyway."

I took a deep breath, pulled up a chair and sat next to the bed. "Can you tell me what happened?"

"What happened is I was hungry, trying to get some food and I thought I could make it down the steps. I was wrong."

"Do you need anything, Mr. Jameson?" A nurse asked entering without knocking.

"I'm fine, Tina." He said with a smile I wanted for myself although didn't deserve.

She nodded and walked out.

"How on earth did you think you were gonna do that in your chair?" I paused. "You could've hurt yourself."

"I did hurt myself."

"I meant killed yourself." I paused. "Russo, we got our problems but I never wanted this for you."

He broke out into laughter. "You have kicked me off of beds, tried to drown me multiple times, starved me and even got my dick hard and left me hanging." He paused. "So please tell me this, if you didn't want it for me, what do you want? Because it ain't love."

I took a deep breath. "I know you lied about how you got like this. And who shot up your house a while back."

He looked at me with wide eyes. "What you talking about now? I said it was them peoples we snatched your house from."

"But that was a lie, Russo."

He moved uneasily in the bed, like he was trying to get comfortable. "And where you hear that from?"

"Does it matter?" I paused. "All that matters is that you wanted me to feel guilty when you first got shot. Guilty enough to move with you in the mansion and leave the house. And to keep the lie alive, and to make me think the drama had nothing to do with the streets, you lied about who shot you up the second time and put you in a wheel chair too."

He shook his head. "My man, Reggie can't hold water to save his life."

"How you know it was Reggie?" I said firmly.

"Who else?"

"Russo, the bottom line is this. The Black Nazi been after you since before we got together. On account of you taking his territory. And it ain't have nothing to do with my family or me. But you lied and that was wrong."

"So all this shit you did to me was because of that?" He glared.

I looked down.

"Wow," he said. "You sure know how to hold a grudge don't you?" He paused. "At least it all makes sense."

"I'm still waiting for an apology, Russo."

"You can wait til you're blue in the face." He said, looking toward the window in the room.

Tears rolled down my cheeks. "You really don't give a fuck about me do you?"

He didn't speak.

"What about our daughter?" I paused. "Do you even care about her?"

"Don't put my daughter in this shit!" He yelled. "Females love mixing kids in the business when it don't concern them."

I moved closer by scooting up the chair. "You are my husband and you can't even say when you're wrong."

He took a deep breath and turned back on the television. It was obvious that he was done with me and that I was done with him. At the end of the day it was clear to see that it was over.

I looked down at my fingers, removed my ring and stood up. "If you don't want it with me, I don't want it with you either." I placed the ring on the table. "Have a nice—"

"Are you Mrs. Jameson?" A black cop followed by two white officers said as he walked into the room.

"Yes," I frowned confused at everything that was happening. "What's this about?"

"You are under arrest for assault on Russo Jameson," he responded and removed handcuffs from his hip. "Face the wall and put your hands up."

I looked over at Russo. My body trembling. My heart rate increased. "What...what is going on?"

"Hands up in the air now, ma'am!" He yelled louder. "Don't make me tell you again."

I turned around and Russo looked away from me as I was arrested. "But I didn't do anything."

"Oh yeah," the cop continued. "Well you tell me why he was thrown down a flight of steps."

I looked at Russo once more. "You did this shit to me when you know I didn't do that?" I cried. "I really hope you feel what it's like to really be without a wife. Get ready, nigga!"

With the cuffs securely around my wrists the officer yanked me out of the room, with me crying all the way.

CHAPTER SEVENTEEN

RUSSO

I was sitting in an empty room that my cousin placed me in at his friends' house in New York feeling like why had I put myself in this situation. There was hardly anything in this place but ants and roaches and I could tell it had been a long time since anybody lived here. Just back from the hospital my arm was sprained and not broken.

Placing my cell phone against my ear I waited for Reggie to answer. "What were you thinking, nigga?"

"Listen, man, please tell me how the fuck was I to know that you were telling her the Black Nazi was her problem?"

"Common sense, Reggie."

"Common sense?!" He yelled. "Are you fucking crazy? All I know was that your wife was in the bathroom hysterical when you came home in that wheel chair. When I asked her why she said you being paralyzed was all her fault. So I cleared shit up."

"But it's obvious if she believed that then I must've told her that. All you had to do is use

118 BY KIM MEDINA

reasonable deductions and keep your mouth closed."

He laughed. "Man, you are whacked the fuck out. If you really think I'm supposed to keep hold of your lies you don't know shit about me."

I took a deep breath. "Did you call the precinct?"

"Yeah, she's being processed but I'll scoop her when I can." He paused. "Did you drop the charges yet?"

"Yeah, but of course they gonna play games and say I gotta let her fall out the system first." I took a deep breath. "This shit wild. All of it, man."

"Nah, what's wild is that you lied on her."

My eyebrows rose. "Come again?"

"Nigga, Amina may have done some foul ass shit but she was no where around you when this happened. And since when you start getting the police involved anyway? You know, with your own case pending, cops is the last thing you need sniffing around you. You not even 'sposed to be out the state."

"I know."

"Then why you lie?"

"Revenge."

He laughed. "Wow, what the fuck type people are we?" He asked in a high-pitched voice. "Everybody in this bitch is tripping hard. And now you living out New York which on my heart I think is a bad move."

"So you would've cleaned my pamper and stuff?" I asked him.

"Russo, I already told you how I feel about that. I ain't keen on niggas shitting and I'm definitely not with looking at another nigga's dick. But I'd prefer to do it myself then have you there. That dude is bad news, Russo. Why don't you give me the address so I can come scoop you. It ain't even know need in being over there now anyway. Amina gone at least for the night."

"Aight," I nodded. "You right. But work on getting my wife out first. Then I'll get the address when Cambridge comes back."

"By the way, who plan on cleaning you up over there?" He asked me.

"I don't even know, man." I said. "I ain't think that much ahead. I been sitting in my shit since I left the hospital yesterday. To make things even worse I can barely move my right arm."

"At least it's sprained and not broken."

"Exactly. The crazy part is, I just had a dream about not being able to use my arm. And I kept obsessing over that shit too. Like thinking about it in the daytime, at night, in my dreams. And now look."

"Amina said the mind is something else if you don't control it. Niggas be thinking they thoughts is lightweight when they ain't."

"Before you get all scholarly with me, tend to your own shit, no pun intended."

The door opened and my cousin came through.

"I got you," Reggie said. "Let me see what's up with the wifey and I'll hit you back."

I hung up and dropped the phone in my pocket. Cambridge sat on the window ledge and tossed a pack of green pampers my way. "Them the only ones I could find. I don't know if they fit."

I shrugged, like it didn't matter even though it did. "So when your man gonna bring the blow up bed I paid for?"

"He said you ain't even have to buy one because his cousin got one at the crib she don't even use."

I frowned. "So where my money at then?"

"Come on, cousin," he said rubbing his hands together. "You know how shit is. I mean, you only gave him a C-Note. But you gonna owe him more if you staying here. Might as well let him keep that to start the tab."

"That's just it, I may only need to stay tonight or at the most two days. I'm going back."

Cambridge nodded. "Is that right?"

"Yeah. I'ma work things out through Reggie."

"You mean that foul ass nigga who be snitching?"

"He don't really be snitching." I sighed. "He just don't be knowing what to say that's all."

"Sounds like snitching to me."

"That's 'cause you don't know him," I said firmly. "But don't worry about it. I won't be in your hair much longer."

"Well you know it ain't no thing for me." He shrugged. "I ain't staying here." He stood up when the door opened and a black chick with a mean scowl on her face stomped inside. "Oh, this my friend I was telling you 'bout. She gonna get you together because you definitely smell foul up in here." He held his nose and laughed. "But I'ma be back."

"Real quick, what's the address to this spot?" I paused as this chick lifted me off the seat and placed me on the hardwood floor like she was a nigga. "I didn't pay attention when we came in. Too much in my head about the wifey and all."

"Don't worry about all that right now, man," he said. "I'll give it to you later."

The woman pulled my pants down, removed my boxers and opened the soiled pamper. She did all of this with a frown on her face and without saying a word. Then she moved my dick with her bare hands, wiped between my ass cheeks with the side of the pamper and then took it off.

My bare ass pressed against the hardwood floor until she opened the pack and put the fresh pamper on. No cleaning and no ointment, which my raw ass was starting to need.

Experiencing the most humiliation in my life I thought about one thing. My wife was right. I was feeling the sting of her not being in the picture and it had only been a day.

CHAPTER EIGHTEEN

TAMIKA

Murphy's house was so plush not only was I relaxed and not thinking about my problems, I realized that it wasn't Reggie who was going to save me after all but Murphy instead.

I had it all wrong.

Besides, he had everything that I need right now in my life.

Looks.

A stable job.

Intelligence.

And more than anything he knew my story. The fact that he was an addict was better in my book because I didn't have to worry about being tempted by liquor being left around the house like I did at home.

The only problem is, I was afraid to go there with him. If we had sex and things changed what if he didn't want me around anymore? This house was not as big as Russo's mansion but with three bedrooms, three levels and a kitchen big enough to live in, a girl could get used to this.

Reggie had been hitting my phone left and right but I knew I was done with him. He could call me all he wanted there was no way on earth I was answering. All he wanted to do was be mean and curse at me like anything about that would make a female want to stay around.

Nah.

I needed this bubble bath I was sitting in. And as many cherries as I could eat because Murphy went to the store to get them and all my other favorites.

And peace.

After soaking for a while I eased out of the tub, walked toward the far end of the bathroom and wrapped my robe around me. When I was done I walked out of the bathroom and stopped short when I heard him talking on the phone in his bedroom, the door cracked open a little.

"Yeah, I know it ain't right but so the fuck what." He laughed. "An eye for an eye."

I moved closer to hear more.

"Nah, man. I made sure of it. I want that nigga to be shook wondering where his wife is." Murphy laughed. "I could've laid the dick down on her too but I got too much respect for sis, know what I mean?" He laughed some more and my heart broke.

Murphy was a snake.

I walked closer to the door and pushed it open. Murphy turned around, looked at me and hung up without saying bye to the caller. "It wasn't what you think it was," he said.

A single tear rolled down my cheek. "Wow. And I thought you were different."

He walked toward me with his hands extended, palms in my direction. "I am different, Cherry. But I—"

"Tamika, my name is Tamika," I said trembling.

"I know and I'm so sorry." He looked down. "Fuck, this looks so bad on my part and it's way off."

"What part is way off? The part that made me think you were my friend when all you wanted to do was get back at Reggie? Or the part where my life is all a game to you. Exactly what part are you talking about?"

He pulled my hands softly, sat on the edge of the bed and positioned me in front of him. Taking a deep breath he said, "I let the ego in me rule my decision making and I was so wrong. But please

126   BY KIM MEDINA

don't let me be the reason your life is out of whack."

I laughed. "You would be arrogant enough to think that wouldn't you?" I frowned.

"Cherry, I—"

I spit in his face. "Nigga fuck you!" Then ran out the door, taking the keys to his truck.

TAMIKA

Tamika had been out doing her thing for two days. After finding out that the reason Drillo could not get a hold of her was because Amina blocked his phone number, she unblocked him and they linked up like nothing had stopped. It didn't take long for her to fall back in drugs and into her old system as a dancer.

Tamika stood in the middle of a crowd of eager men. Carmelo, the groom, excitedly rubbed the sweat from his palm as he anticipated the cutie blessing his lap with a dance. Besides, for the past few months everyone had been talking about the girl who could move her body like a snake and seeing as though he would be a married man in a few days, he wanted to share his moment with her.

When the bass from 'Bodak Yellow' thumped through the speakers, Tamika swirled her hips and waist as if it would twist off at any moment. She wanted him to know she was with it all. She could feel Carmelo's eyes on her and could even see the fresh stiffness rising in his pants. Carefully she moved toward him before sitting on his lap and pushing and twirling into him as if he were her husband.

"Don't move, sexy," he said in her ear, his breath tart from too much drinking. "I'ma 'bout to bust and you feel so fucking good. Damn, man."

She continued to dance on him but said, "I don't mind all that, but you gotta give my brother over there extra before you let loose, otherwise it's just the dance." She moved to get up and he forcefully put her back into his lap, waving Drillo over quickly.

"What you need, man?" Drillo said into his ear, to be heard over the music.

"Extra," Carmelo said, reaching into his pocket, handing Drillo a fifty. "I'ma need that to happen."

Having seen the exchange, his friends cheered him on excitedly knowing he was about to risk it all. "You got that, but you don't want yours off now right?" Drillo said as Tamika continued to work as he handled his business. "Meet us in the room in about ten minutes."

Carmelo glared. "Alright, but don't be fuckin' with my money. It wouldn't be good for your life."

"Ain't nobody messing with you, man," Drillo said. "This your night." He slapped him on the back and Tamika got up.

"Hurry up because I'ma be waiting," she said winking at him. "I'm going into the bathroom to freshen up."

She and Drillo walked into the bathroom and grabbed the clothes she stashed in the tub. Next she quickly slipped into her jeans and white t-shirt. For the night they had already collected $450, courtesy of her dancing skills and now it was time to bounce.

While Carmelo's friends poured tequila down his throat in celebration, Tamika and Drillo slipped out the house, breaking the future deal and escaping with the tips and $50.00 additional bucks. Thirty minutes later they copped from their regular dealer and was getting high in a run down motel room in Baltimore City.

Sitting on the edge of the bed, next to the curtains, Tamika grabbed the lighter from her purse to get high.

"Hurry the fuck up," Drillo said sitting next to her. "You taking too long."

"Calm down!" Tamika scolded him. "This from me dancing not you."

The moment she ignited the lighter, a huge flame flew from it and connected to the curtain. Within seconds the material went up in flames along with Tamika's braids. As she dropped the pipe to slap at her face and arms, in an effort to put out the fire, Drillo picked up the pipe attempting to smoke.

Searing pain took over her body and before long she was engulfed. Thinking on her feet she managed to stumble outside and that's when an unlikely neighbor saved her.

BY KIM MEDINA

CHAPTER NINETEEN
REGGIE

I walked into the hospital room where my wife was and when I saw her I almost wanted to dip back out. My temples throbbed. She was covered from head to toe in gauze and her eyes were closed. What had me a new kind of mad was when I saw her brother there. He was sitting in a chair in the room.

I walked close to him so that only he could hear me. "Listen, I don't wanna do this in front of my wife but—"

He stood up. "I'm leaving. But I'll be back. Believe that."

I was about to steal him in the face when, "Reggie, is that you?" She said in a low voice.

I turned around, walked over to the bed and watched Drillo walk out. "Yeah, it's me."

I saw a tear well up in her eyes, the only part of her face visible. "I'm so sorry about this."

I put my hand over her gauze-covered hand and she winced. I quickly pulled it back. "I'm sorry. I...I don't know what to say, bae. What happened?" I paused. "Doc said you 90% burned."

She nodded. "I know. But it's mostly second degree burns so I shouldn't be too scarred."

"But what happened, Mika?" I asked. "Why you catching up with Drillo again anyway?"

"I don't want to talk about that part." She took a deep breath. "I mean, I asked him to leave my room and he wouldn't go." She paused. "But I'm done with drugs now. This shit right here—"

"Stop it. Just stop it, 'Mika." I wiped my hand down my face. "Look, I gotta...I gotta go." I stormed out, leaving her alone.

REGGIE

Amina looked hard when I picked her up but I understood why too. She'd spent four days in a holding cell even though they got word that Russo had dropped the charges a long time ago. And he stopped answering his cell phone so I don't know what was going on with him either.

"You mad at me?" I asked when we were five minutes from the house.

She looked at me and shook her head. "Nah, if anything you should be mad at me for saying something to Russo."

I waved the air with my free hand. "Man, fuck that. How was I supposed to know the nigga was lying to you? You was crying and I didn't want you sad about shit that wasn't even on you." I shrugged. "Call me wrong but that's just me."

She looked at me, smiled and nodded her head. "Thank you. I think that's why my mother wanted you for us. For me."

When we made it to the house she went upstairs and I sat on the sofa and ate a ham and cheese sandwich. I was about to turn on the TV when she called out. "Reggie!"

I put the paper plate down and ran upstairs. She was standing in front of the closet in her bathrobe. "What's up?"

"The towels are on the top shelf again," she said pointing in the linen closet.

"Ah, fuck, I'm sorry," I said shaking my head before walking behind her. I reached over her head and tried to grab a fluffy yellow one. "I keep forgetting not to put it that high up."

"What are you doing?" She yelled, pushing me away.

"What you talking about?" I frowned.

"Why you hard?"

I looked down at myself and shook my head. "Amina, on everything that shit just happened. My mind is all fucked up and, and, as you can see one thing led to another. Sometimes it happens to me when I'm stressed."

Suddenly she rushed up to me and pounded me repeatedly in the chest with her fist. I took the first three blows but everything after started stinging my chest. So I wrapped my arms around her until the energy she had was gone.

Finally she cried heavily in my arms, as I rocked her. "I hate him," she cried harder. "I fucking hate him so much."

"I know," I said. "But we gonna be alright. All of us."

She continued to cry until suddenly she stopped. Looking up at me she placed her hands on my face and stood on her tiptoes. Before I knew it her lips were pressed against mine and my dick was firmly against her lower belly. By now I was fully aware of it and it ached so badly it itched and I thought it would explode if I didn't get relief.

I lifted her off her feet and she wrapped her legs around my waist. It gave me instant access. I could smell the mustiness of her pussy due to being in the holding cell for so long and that turned me on even more. Before I knew it my jeans were at my ankles and my dick was in her pussy.

"Ahhhhhhh..." I said as my mouth hung open. She was so tight, so warm and so wet. It made me wonder if the towel thing was just a ploy to get me upstairs from the break.

Was she a sex fiend too?

"Fuck me, Reggie," she said sucking my bottom lip as I carried her to her room. "Fuck this pussy because I need you so badly."

Once inside I laid her on the bed, pushed her legs further apart and raised my hips before drilling up and down slowly. Wanting the shit to last I raised my hips again and left just the tip inside as she begged me to come back down.

The way she looked. Smelled and sounded it made me wonder why we hadn't fucked before. It's obvious we were a perfect match by the way my dick melted inside of her heat.

Finally, unable to take it anymore, I put half of my weight on her body, her breasts pushing against my chest as she swirled her hips and sucked my ear.

"You feel so good," she moaned. "Please, please don't stop. I need you, Reggie. Please."

We fucked for eight hours straight, only taking breaks to grab a quick drink and something to eat in between. Yeah the shit was wrong. And yes guilt set in after we took a shower only to fuck again.

But for now it was like we were a couple.

And this was our home.

So in the moment it was alright.

And our little secret.

CHAPTER TWENTY

RUSSO

I'm seated in my chair with a dart in my hand. Cambridge and Luke, the dude who owned the house were standing beside me. When I felt I was ready I threw the dart at the board on the wall and landed a bulls eye once again.

"Damn!" Cambridge said covering his mouth. "My man in wheels but he be landing them mothafuckas don't he?"

Luke, a big nigga of about four hundred pounds sucked his teeth. He wasn't happy about it at all. He walked over to the small table, grabbed a dollar bill tightly wrapped and snorted a line of coke. "Fuck outta here." He wiped his nose.

"Oh you mad?" Cambridge laughed, pushing his arm. "Don't get mad, my guy. We just having fun."

See Cambridge may have thought he was funny but he had a way of annoying the hell out of people. I told him several times before that at some point the jokes have got to stop. But he be too interested in getting a good laugh to see when a nigga was ready to blow.

"Now you gotta pay my cousin since you lost the bet," Cambridge said pushing me.

"Man, how I look paying a nigga some bread who for real owes me?" Luke said.

"That is true," Cambridge said all of a sudden.

The room got quiet, as they both looked at me, like I had dollar signs posted on my face. It had been about three days since I came here and I'm pretty sure that I'm a hostage. My cousin didn't tell me and neither did Luke, but it was obvious something was going on. What I didn't know was why.

"Look, all you gotta do is give me the address and my people will come scoop me." I said. "I'll be out of your hair with no problem."

"But you already been here for almost a week." Luke said. "What about that? You owe me for real for real for at least a month's stay. Not to mention I had my girl wiping yah ass and shit."

That broad was his girl?

"Look, I can't do nothing because ya'll not letting me go," I said louder. "Listen, my friend Reggie already on standby. All you have to do is give me back my phone and let me bounce."

"Nah, you see, I'm not gonna be able to do that." Luke said. "'Cause your cousin here said that nigga is foul. And in your condition and all, I wouldn't feel comfortable letting you get away like that." He smiled. "Sooooo, you have to find another source."

"Again, how am I gonna do that since you niggas took my phone and shit?"

"Cousin, I know you got some bread," Cambridge said. "All you gotta do is tell me where it's at and I'll scoop it and take you home." He said rubbing his hands together. "It's that simple."

I shook my head. "My wife told me you was a foul ass nigga."

He gritted his teeth. "That's what she said?"

I nodded yes.

Cambridge walked toward the wall, removed the darts one by one. Next he turned toward me and threw the first one my way. It landed in my arm. "Ouch!"

I tried to get away from him but he tossed another and it hit my leg.

"Fuck is you doing?" I yelled while Luke busted out laughing in the background.

"Just having a little fun?" Cambridge said throwing another one. "Why? What it look like I'm doing?"

TAMIKA

I was sitting up on the edge of the bed when Gina walked into the door. She had been clean all this time but as you can tell from my situation that didn't matter. But it didn't stop her from thinking Reggie would want a relationship by seeing her, especially since she was the one who helped put the fire out on me when I walked out the building for help. Because Drillo was too worried about getting high to even care.

"How are you?" She asked coming inside, looking behind her every so often.

"Gina, I'm fine. But Reggie and Amina are on their way to get me. If they see you they won't like it. You have to leave. Please."

"I will, I will," She nodded looking behind her again. "But I need you to talk to him for me. I miss my son and you promised you'd put in a word."

I took a deep breath. "Look at me, Gina. I'm wrapped up in gauze from head to toe and Reggie and my sister are gonna have to deal with this for a little while. The last thing I want to do is put this on them too. Give him some time. He'll reach out. I have your number."

She smirked and took a step back. "I should've let you burn to death."

"Get the fuck out!"

She smiled. "I'm leaving now, but I'll be back. You can believe that."

Fifteen minutes later Reggie and Amina were there and they walked me out the door. I sat in the front seat but I would've preferred the back because the energy was way off in the car. It's like they didn't want me to be home. I guess they were tired of having to come to my rescue and the guilt was weighing on me.

"I'm sorry." I said to them both. "About all of this. But I'ma stay clean this time. Trust me. This shit right here has gone way too far. I mean look at me."

"We just wanna get you home," Amina said. "Nothing more, nothing less."

Reggie turned to look at her and then focused back on me. "Nah, I'm not letting her off so easy this time. I'm sick of you and this reckless shit. You could've been killed."

"Reggie, please," Amina said softly touching his shoulder. "Please don't talk to her like that."

He looked back at her again before focusing on the road. "Look, I'm sorry, Tamika. I know you didn't mean for this to happen but this is what I was afraid of. And I'm not running after you no more. If you wanna stay clean then you gonna have to prove it. That's all I'm gonna say."

BY KIM MEDINA

CHAPTER TWENTY-ONE

AMINA

This was so wrong but it felt so right.

Don't misunderstand me, I know this fucked up on many levels but Reggie and I have a way about working out our problems. A way that won't get in the way of other things. Like his marriage to my sister and my marriage to a man who won't even pick up the phone when Reggie and me call him.

With my hands planted on the kitchen sink, Reggie pounded at me from behind. His stiff dick feels like a relaxing massage from the inside and already all of my problems go away. When I feel my body heating up and clit tingle a little I know I'm about to scream out in pleasure. Thank goodness for Reggie because he slapped his hand over my mouth and continued to fuck me until we both reached our moment.

"You about to get us late," he said in a heavy whisper as he put on his pants after we both finished. "We ain't in this bitch no more by ourselves."

"I know, I know, and I'm gonna miss that shit too," I nodded while pulling up my panties and straightening my pajamas. "But she still sleep right?"

"Yeah, before I came down here she was knocked out with her mouth open. Them pills they gave her be having her done for the day. I swear I hope they don't do more harm to her than good with her addiction." He wiped his hand down his face. "What have we gotten ourselves into?"

I shrugged. "I don't know," I said under my breath.

"Amina, if you wanna stop right now I'll do it. Trust me, the last thing I wanna do is hurt you and definitely not my wife. It's just that..." He moved closer, snaked his hand around the lower part of my neck and brought my face to his. "...I need you." He kissed me softly.

I nodded. "And I need you too but what are we doing, Reggie? I mean really."

He walked away and leaned against the wall across from the stove. "Fuck if I know?" He laughed once. "If you would've told me that we would be doing this I wouldn't believe you."

"Never in a million years."

"Never in a million years," I repeated as I continued to stare at him. Why did he have to be so fine? So perfect? "Do you...do you still love her?"

He nodded yes. "It's hard for you to see now, Amina, I get that. But Tamika...she...she just knows how to speak to that part of me that makes me want to fight for her."

I looked down. "I get it."

"Please don't catch feelings for me."

My eyebrows rose. "Nigga, you don't catch feelings for me."

"I didn't mean it that way." He moved closer and grabbed my hand. "I didn't...I..." He took a deep breath. "What the fuck are we doing?" He said again before laughing.

This time we both laughed just as Tamika walked into the kitchen. I felt like I had shitted on myself except I didn't. She looked at Reggie holding my hand and I just knew our secret was out.

"Good, you're up," Reggie said still holding me. Why hadn't he let me go? "Come over here, Tamika." Tamika walked over to us slowly. "I was just telling your sister that I really believe this is gonna be it for you. That after all of this you gonna change." He paused and grabbed her hand that was covered in gauze. "I didn't want to bring this to you, Tamika but Russo ain't been answering the phone and Amina been real upset lately. And I was consoling her and telling her that everything gonna be okay."

This nigga good with this lying shit and that makes him creepy.

"Yeah, I'm just worried about you and Russo." I said hoping I wouldn't ruin it. "But we got to make shit right around here first."

He finally released me and hugged her softly. "We need you to be strong, Tamika. And drug free. Can you do that for us?"

She nodded a few times walked over to me and pulled us into a three-person hug. The whole time I'm feeling like the biggest snake of them all.

REGGIE

We just finished eating and it was going on day eight of me not speaking to Russo and I made

BY KIM MEDINA

some decisions. But first I had to make sure Tamika didn't suspect anything was going on with me and her sister and so far it looked like she didn't. But she had a way of holding onto shit until she was ready to blow.

Despite being covered in gauze I could tell she smiled. "What's that for?"

"I can tell you love me."

"Yeah, I do," I placed my hand on her thigh. "And I'm fighting for us."

She nodded. "I can feel it. Before this happened to me you were barely home but now you're here every night, not searching the streets or looking for something that's not out there."

My heart thumped. Of course I didn't stay out late anymore. My wife was in the house and her sister was giving me that good pussy with no questions asked. Basically my stress problems were over.

"I haven't been running around lately but I am going to have to make some moves today."

"Why, what's up?"

"I don't have a good feeling about not hearing from Russo. Don't get me wrong, before he left him and Amina were going at it but...I got the impression that he wanted to come home. So why ain't he calling?"

"Well I don't care if he ever come back." She paused.

I frowned. "Why you say that?"

"He had my sister locked up."

I nodded. "I get all that but they both did a lot to each other, Tamika. And he made that right by dropping the charges. It's two sides to a situation. You know that."

She placed her hand over mine. "I know."

I took a deep breath. "Well, let me hit these streets. I'll bring ya'll something back nice."

"I'm sure me and Amina would like that."

I winked, grabbed the keys to my car and walked out.

CHAPTER TWENTY-TWO
RUSSO

"Cambridge, you gotta stop this shit, man," I pleaded with him. They had me lying on a palette they made for me on the floor with some thin ass sheets. He took my wheel chair and my clothes, forcing me to lay in my own piss and shit with nothing but a thick quilt covering me. "I'm your blood and you and your boy have kicked me and beat me in the face...this wrong."

Cambridge smiled and leaned against the wall. "Is that right?"

"Yes! What have I ever done to you to deserve any of this shit? Because I'm confused right now."

He sucked his teeth and rubbed his hands together. "You remember the summer of '99?"

I looked to my right and back at him. I had a lot of personal shit going on in my life at that time but nothing that stood out hard enough to deserve all this. "Nah...I don't."

"Well I do." There was a smile on his face that went away slowly. "It was the summer that I realized you really have to worry about yourself."

"Man, you gotta be clearer." I used my good arm to scoot to the wall and leaned against it. "Please."

"You were ten and I was nine." He smiled. "You used to come by my mama's house in DC with all this money. And I used to be so excited because I got to tell everybody that this was my cousin from Baltimore." He rubbed his hands together and looked up. "Because every other summer you came we were so close."

"I know...really close."

"But this summer, the one I'm talking about now, you were different. I ain't never have no money like you but that didn't bother you before. So what my clothes were dirty. That's what you used to tell niggas who laughed at me anyway. But that summer, you didn't even want me sitting next to you."

"I don't remember."

"I know you don't." He nodded. "Anyway this one day you were telling my moms about all the shit you had back at home." He smiled. "You the first nigga I knew with the Gameboy Color. And all I wanted to do was sit next to you and watch you play it on my couch. I wasn't even gonna ask

to touch it because I felt like I ain't deserve to."
He paused. "Do you know what you said?"

"No."

"You told me to get my dusty ass away from you because you ain't want me getting your Rocawear short set dirty."

I looked around confused because I still didn't remember. That was during the time Wesley and Peter came around. They would pick their favorite young niggas from the block and force us to do stuff to them or to let them do stuff to us for money. Back then Wesley was a big dealer so I stayed with new clothes and money. But for real I would've given it all up for peace of mind.

"My friends were there. My girlfriend at the time and even my mother. And guess what, they all laughed." He shook his head. "It took me three years just to get the nickname, Dusty off of me. Lost my girl and everything after you left." He paused. "As a matter of fact one nigga called me Dusty last year. He ain't here no more."

"Man, if I—"

"Don't say you sorry." He paused. "Because you don't mean it." He peeled himself off the wall, walked up to me and kicked me in the face. "You got until the end of the day to tell me where it's at." He paused. "No money. No life."

CAMBRIDGE

Cambridge walked out the room and up to Luke who was sitting with his mean faced girlfriend, doing lines of coke.

"So what's the status?" Luke asked.

"He ain't talking."

"Fuck!" Luke said standing up before walking away. "I'm starting to think your ass lying." He said pointing at Cambridge. He wiped the coke residue off his nose and licked it.

"Nah, I'm telling you, my cousin sitting on paper. He just ain't been inspired enough to give it up."

Mean Face Girl smiled. "If you give me some time alone with him I could probably come up with a plan."

"What that mean?" Cambridge frowned.

"Does it matter, nigga?" Luke said. "Because whether you know it or not, we at the point of no return."

Cambridge glared. "I know you not talking about—"

"Murder," Mean Face Girl said.

"Nah, I'm not about to—"

Luke rushed up to Cambridge with his belly and shoved him against the wall. "You not about to what?"

"I'ma need you to back the fuck up." Cambridge said softly.

"And if I don't?" Luke laughed. "Just what the fuck do you plan to—

CLICK. CLICK.

Slowly Luke's eyes moved down to the not one but two guns being pointed at his dick. "How the fuck did you get them out so quick?" Luke said in a low voice.

"Back the fuck up off me." Cambridge said again. "I won't ask a third time."

Luke moved backwards and raised his hands in the air. "I ain't mean nothing by it."

Mean Face Girl walked up. "Look, I know he your people but even you ain't dumb enough to think that after he gives us this money that he gonna let us get away with all this," she said to Cambridge.

"She's right," Luke said.

"But he's my blood."

And just what the fuck did you think would happen?" Luke continued. "That we would shake him down and he would just go on about life?"

"Nah...I..." Cambridge scratched his head, the words lost in this throat.

"We gotta get that money and then finish him off. It's the only way."

CHAPTER TWENTY-THREE
REGGIE

Amina and me were putting our clothes on in the shed behind the house. Tamika was inside and it was getting harder to find places to be together and I needed her more. Amina was the only reason I wasn't out in these streets because fucking with her felt...right.

"Did you find out anything on Russo?" I zipped my pants.

"Nah, his aunt says she doesn't know where that house is that Cambridge be at. But that she would keep her eyes and ears open for me."

She looked downward. "Hey, hey, hey, don't worry." I raised her chin. "I'll find him." I put back on my belt.

She smiled. "Thank you."

I winked and when we were both dressed I looked over at her again. "You ready?"

She nodded.

"Okay, I'ma leave first and then you come in the house about ten minutes later." I was about to walk out when she softly touched my arm. "Let's go."

"We have to stop this," she said.

"Amina, please don't do this."

"Don't do what? Fuck you in the shed out back of the house because we being trifling?"

"Nah, don't take yourself from me when you know I need it." I paused. "Don't you understand what this does for me?"

She laughed softly. "You my sister's husband."

"So what!" I said louder than I wanted. "I love her and you love her too. And we ain't trying to hurt her or nobody else but—"

"If she ever finds out I will lose her forever." She said. "Even if she talks to me again she'll probably get back on drugs and we'll lose her to the street."

"I won't let that happen."

"But how can you be sure, Reggie?"

I scratched my head. I needed to find the right words to explain how much this, whatever it was, meant for me. "I'm falling in love with you."

Her eyes widened and she shook her head softly from left to right. "No...no...no...you said we couldn't do that. Told me not to fall for you and I told you not to fall for me."

"I know." I grabbed her hands. "And I get that. But now it's too late."

156   BY KIM MEDINA

"Reggie, we can't be...we can't..."

"We?" I said looking into her eyes.

"I meant...I meant....you."

"Nah, you feel the same way don't you?" I paused as I held her hand. "You feel just like me but it's just wrong to say it."

"Reggie, this can never work."

I grabbed her and pulled her closer. "Do you love me or not?"

It felt like forever for her to answer and for some reason her eyes and the way she held her body told me the answer would be the same as mine. "No."

"No?" I repeated.

"No, I don't love you."

"Well I don't believe you," I said.

She tried to walk around me and out the door. I gripped her up, pulled her in and kissed her. Off the break she wrapped her arms around my neck and kissed me back. "I love you...I love you too," she said. "I can't lie."

And just like that, we were down for round two.

TAMIKA

I was tired of sitting around the house doing nothing. Reggie and Amina were only God knows where and I felt useless since I was burned. Yes I was in pain but it didn't hurt as much and I was already able to take the bandages off my face and hands. I just had to keep them clean that's all.

So I decided I would at least help with the housework. First I started wiping the counters in the kitchen and then I emptied old food out of the refrigerator and cabinets. When I was done I looked down at the kitchen floor and was disgusted because it hadn't been done in over a month. I decided to get the mop from the shed and clean it up.

But when I looked out through the back door I noticed the shed was shaking. "What the fuck was going on?"

Running back into the living room to grab my shoes I decided to check. But when I came back to the back door Murphy was standing there, looking at me. "What...what are you doing here?"

158   BY KIM MEDINA

"I had to see you." He said through wired teeth.

"But I gave you your truck already." I said frantically.

"I know but…"

I opened the door, pulled him in and rushed him to the living room. "Well why are you here?" I asked. "Are you trying to get me killed? He won't stand for this. You know it."

"What happened to you?" He asked staring deeper into my eyes. "Did he do this?"

"No…and why do you care anyway?" I crossed my arms until the sting from my burns hit me and I uncrossed them again. "You are not my friend, Murphy. Please stop faking like you are."

"Okay, I know I was wrong."

"Wrong is an understatement."

"Yes it is. But I wanted you to know something from the heart; I really, really care about you. More than I can explain. And all I want is your recovery." He paused. "I know you can't see it in yourself to forgive me now but I won't stop trying."

I shook my head. "Why should I believe you?" I shrugged. "Huh?"

He walked closer to me and smiled. "Because even though you know that nigga would break me in two if he saw me in here you let me in the house anyway. And a part of you loves that I'm willing to risk danger to prove how much I care."

I looked down. Maybe he was right. "But why me? I ain't got nothing. I ain't nobody."

"You somebody to me. And when you finish doing whatever this is with him I think you'll finally see."

CHAPTER TWENTY-FOUR

AMINA

I got to get away from this man.

I had the craziest ideas in my head on how to make it happen too. I thought about him dying. Him getting into a car accident. Even him finding someone else and leaving. And every time the ideas entered my head I quickly wished them away, knowing that I had the tendency to make the craziest shit happen. I didn't really want him dead. I just wanted a decision to be made for me, to tear us apart instead of how it is now.

After our round two we decided we were pushing it by still being in the shed. "Okay, I'ma leave out first." He said smiling. "You after me."

"Are you sure, because last time you said it and..."

"Stop talking before I slide in you again." He winked. "And you know I will."

When he opened the door I backed up against the wall and buttoned my shirt so nobody would see me.

"Tamara!" He yelled.

"What you doing?" I whispered. "She's gonna hear us!"

"That girl is here!" He said before taking off running.

When the door opened wider I saw her looking at us, pointing. But when he gave chase she ran too. Reggie dug into his pocket tossed me the keys and said, "Get my truck. I'ma follow this bitch!" He ran faster after her as she took off around the front of the house.

AMINA

I pulled up to the place where Reggie told me to wait in his truck. Ten minutes later he approached and was out of breath. "I couldn't find her."

I looked ahead. "So what...what do you think she's gonna do?"

"I don't know," he said looking into my eyes. "But she definitely saw us come out of that shed and me fixing my pants. I know that for sure." He sighed. "And that broad got away with herself."

162 BY KIM MEDINA

"So you fucked her too," I said shaking my head.

"You know her?"

"Of course." I took a deep breath and leaned back into the seat. "She's Russo's ex-girlfriend. When I was trying to see what I was going to do about our relationship, in the beginning, she stepped to us when we were at a restaurant one day. All I could think about at the time was how much prettier than me she was."

"That's not true."

"Then what is it, Reggie? Why are men drawn to that bitch? Tell me that?"

He shrugged. "Because she's easy."

I laughed. "Wow."

"Not...I mean...not like you trying to make it out to be."

"You mean not like me trying to make it out to be by fucking you whenever you want in the same house I share with my sister?" I paused. "Because if you ask me it doesn't get easier than that."

"Fuck! I'm not saying that."

"But you did."

"Amina, I'm begging you not to do this to me."

"Do what?"

"Be deep." He paused. "I like what we got going on. Our thing makes shit easier for the both of us, not worst." He took a deep breath. "And I been stop smashing that bitch when I saw she wasn't worth it." He grabbed my hand. "But, Amina I swear, I can't see not doing this with you."

When his cell phone rang he took it out his pocket and looked at the screen. "Who is it?"

"Her." He hit the button. "Where you at, Tamara?"

"Well, well, well." She said slyly. "So that's why you didn't wanna fuck with me no more."

"See, told you I didn't want that bitch," he said in a low voice to me.

I smiled.

"What you talking about?" He asked her on the phone.

"I'm talking about seeing you come out of the shed fixing your pants while she was fixing her shirt." She paused. "You's about a nasty bitch. Wait till I tell Russo!"

"Listen, I'm asking you not to do that." He begged.

"And why should I listen to you? The man who treated me like shit when all I wanted to do was make him feel good?"

"Can we talk?" He said. "Please."

"So now you wanna talk?"

"Yes. Listen, what you think you saw you didn't and I just wanna explain it to you a little. That's all."

"Nah, what you want me to do is keep your secret so you can keep fucking your sister-in-law while forgetting all about me."

"Tamara—"

"Tamara nothing!" She yelled cutting him off. "What I want is you at my house in two hours with a bag, preparing to stay over night."

He frowned. "You know I can't do that."

"Are you sure, Reggie? Because I'm still in the neighborhood. I could always swing by and—"

"Okay!" He yelled at the phone.

"Okay what?" She said slyly.

"Okay I'm coming...just...just..." he took a deep breath. "Just give me some time to figure out what I'm going to tell my wife."

"Tell your wife whatever you want. As a matter of fact get your slutty sister-in-law to help out. Because from now on when I want the dick or the lips you are gonna do exactly what I tell you." She laughed. "Them bitches gonna have to understand that you are not gonna be just serving them up anymore. Because I need mine too." She hung up.

He tossed the phone in his lap. "This went to a whole different level now," he said to me.

"I know." I said. "So what we gonna do?"

He turned his body to look at me. "I don't know how you feel but I'm ready to go all the way. What 'bout you?"

I placed my hand on his. "What's the plan?"

CHAPTER TWENTY-FIVE

TAMIKA

I was standing in the living room looking out the door when April finally pulled up. She parked the car in front of the house and walked around to get Naverly before carrying her inside. Naverly looked so happy and it always amazed me how babies could be so free spirited despite the adults around them breaking down. Or did they know what was happening and unconsciously choose smiling to make things all better? To convince us that they were clueless.

"Hey, Tamika, I got here fast as I could." She said walking through the door. "Can I hug you or will it hurt."

"It would hurt."

"Hey, aunt 'Mika." Naverly said when April put her down. "Are you okay?"

I bent down and kissed her cheek. "I'm fine. But why don't you go up to your room and play. I wanna talk to April." I smiled.

"Okay," she said happily before darting up the steps.

When she was gone April put her purse on the table and we both walked to the sofa before sitting down. "So talk to me. What's up?"

"I think something may have happened to Reggie."

She frowned. "How you figure?"

I took a deep breath. "Well, earlier today I was cleaning the kitchen and I saw something happening in the shed. But when I put my shoes on to check it out my sponsor came over. After he left I checked and it was empty."

"Your sponsor?"

"My drug sponsor. He's supposed to help me through staying clean but...as you know it's not working."

She took a deep breath. "Yeah. I heard that's how you hurt yourself. Smoking the pipe."

"April, I'm so confused. I thought Reggie was supposed to be there to save me and then I thought it was this dude but...it's all a joke."

April smiled. "You know I have a boyfriend right?"

"No, I didn't." I grinned nudging her leg. "You got a picture?" She removed her phone from her purse and showed me an image of this chocolate man with a smooth goatee and baldhead. "Wow. He's everything."

But she nodded like she could take him or leave him. "He's cool."

"I don't get it. You don't seem too happy."

She put her phone down and sighed. "I care about him a lot. But before I could give him even part of me I had to find out who I was first, Tamika. I took some time to find out what I liked to eat. What things I liked to do when I wasn't at work. How to pleasure myself."

"Without him?" I frowned.

"Yes."

"Ewww...fuck would you want to do that for?"

She laughed. "I know it sounds gross but it's only because we were taught that we can't do anything without a man. Now don't get me wrong, I love Blake but he ain't messing with who I'm building on the inside. He can add to it, which he does, but he is not allowed to make my shit worse. I had to spend some time alone so I could spend some time with someone else."

I sat back in the sofa. "But how do you do that?"

"Well," she sighed. "First you gotta let shit burn."

My eyes widened.

"Not in that way," she said extending her hand. "I'm not talking about the physical burns you've gone through but the mental ones you not ready to deal with." She paused. "It means when Reggie acts up, instead of responding with violence or anger you sit with it for a little while and see how it feels. Ask yourself what makes you angry about him acting up. When you have your answer ask yourself if you think he's capable of changing, even if you are misreading his actions. You ask question after question until you find out why you are really upset." She paused. "And do you know what the answer always is? That you aren't feeling loved."

"So how do I get him to make me feel that way?"

"You make yourself feel that way first." She said softly. "You let the mental shit burn and then when you get through it, because you will, you'll find out that you like taking long walks by yourself. That you can eat a meal alone. That you like the sound of silence because it relaxes you minus all the drama." Suddenly she smiled brightly. "Once that shit happens, I'm telling you, it's like you get a whole new set of glasses to look at the world with. You may even find out that Reggie ain't the one for you."

"I don't think I can do it."

She shrugged. "Then get ready to feel and look like this over and over again. And you are looking bad, cousin. Because I'ma tell you something else too. There is nothing more attractive, or sexy, then a woman who loves herself."

DRILLO

After just robbing a dope boy on the corner with a fake gun, Drillo took off running before dipping into an abandoned house. He had robbed the same dude repeatedly and already had a place to go invisible as he ran around the neighborhood looking for him.

Sitting in a dark corner in the living room, he removed his pipe and took out the stolen crack rocks. Placing them into the pipe he lit it and inhaled deeply.

And then something happened.

Something different than the things that happened before. He heard them getting closer. Their yells loud and violent. But an extreme peace came over him that he could not explain. And in that instant, although his body was filled with drugs he had a clairvoyant moment.

"God, please forgive me for all my sins." He said leaning against the wall. "And watch over my sisters."

Looking out ahead he heard footsteps in the distance and he knew it was all over.

"There he go right there!" The dope boy said, accompanied by two other men.

The angry dealer removed the weapon from his waist just as Drillo closed his eyes and BOOM!

He was killed instantly with a single bullet to the head.

CHAPTER TWENTY-SIX
REGGIE

Tamara was on my dick as I pumped into her slowly. Although I was glaring at this dumb bitch she didn't seem to notice. It didn't matter to her that I didn't want to be with her. As far as she was concerned she won and that was enough to make her cum.

"Yes...yes...yes...," she said as she threw her head back and fell into my chest. "That was...um...so...so good." She kissed my arm and my skin crawled. "How do you know how to work that dick so good?"

I shrugged.

She giggled.

"Come on, Reggie. You can't still be that mad at me."

"Why shouldn't I? You blackmailing me. Ain't nobody trying to be here."

She sat up on the bed and looked down at me. "Wow, you really are gonna act like you this mad."

"It ain't an act no more." I sat up and looked at her. My back against her brass headboard.

"You can't make a nigga wanna be with you. It don't work like that."

She shrugged. "I don't have to make you wanna be with me. I just have to make you wanna fuck me which I've done with your little secret." She giggled and leaned against me.

I pushed her off and got out of bed. Grabbing my Black & Mild's off the TV I lit one and leaned against the wall.

"Awww, Reggie, don't be a sore loser," she said crawling toward me. "I just wanna play with you a little while longer and then I'll let you go. I promise."

I inhaled and blew smoke down at her. "You a stupid bitch you know that?"

She laughed. "But I'm a sexy one too." She got on her knees and placed my moist dick between her lips and sucked again until I was hard.

I hated that my body kept responding to this shit. Before I knew it she was drinking my nut for the second time that day.

"Mmmmm...sweet." She wiped the corners of her mouth with her fingertips and I pushed her out the way with the bottom of my foot to the face. She laughed as I sat on the edge of the bed before she crawled between my legs again.

174   BY KIM MEDINA

"Let me be all things to you."

"Right now the only thing you are to me is annoying," I said before blowing more smoke down in her face and putting the black and mild out on her mattress.

"And that will change over time."

"Never. It will never change."

Suddenly the door opened and she jumped up when she saw Amina walking inside with a gun aimed at her. Relieved, I got up and walked over to Amina before leaning against the doorway. I smiled at how scared Tamara looked now.

"What's happening?" Tamara asked crawling on the bed by the headboard. "Why is this bitch here?"

"You know what's going on. Today is your last day on earth." I walked over to my grey sweatpants and slipped into them, before sliding on my t-shirt. "Any last words?"

"Please don't do this," She sobbed.

I laughed. "Do you really think I would go through all the trouble to unlock the door. Fuck you more times than I felt like doing, all not to get rid of you?"

"But...but I won't say anything. I promise." She said. "Please don't do this."

I looked at Amina. "Do it." Amina held the gun firmly but it just trembled in her hand. "Amina, do that shit." I said softly. She still didn't move. "If you don't she will say something. Trust me. She'll—"

"I already left a message on Russo's phone."

My heart thumped. "What you just say?"

"I said I already left a message," Tamara continued. "He knows about you too."

Amina's hand dropped and the gun lowered.

"You're lying." I said.

She smiled slyly. "Am I?"

I snatched the gun from Amina's hand, pointed it at Tamara and pulled the trigger. Her body slumped to the right before she died, her blood spilling onto the mattress.

Amina passed out and I caught her right before she hit the floor.

Fifteen minutes later we were sitting on the floor and she had come to. "What happened?"

"You don't remember?" I asked rubbing her head.

She nodded and looked over at Tamara's corpse. "Now I do."

I took a deep breath. "What are we gonna do?" I paused. "If it's true that Russo knows then..."

"We both in trouble," she said. "Do you...do you think that Russo...what you think he gonna do if he find out?"

I took a deep breath. "Amina, I don't even know. For real. The dude ain't been answering my phone calls for days. Even if she left a message it doesn't mean he got it." I shrugged. "I think we gotta deal with what's in front of us right now." I looked on the bed and at the body.

She looked at me. "What we gonna do with her?"

"Leave her right here."

"But won't they know it was us?"

"I'll wipe my DNA off of her and my fingerprints too." I paused. "Did you park where I told you too?"

She nodded yes.

"Then we should be fine."

She looked down. "This is the second time in my life something like this has happened. That I was around a murder."

"With who?"

"The girl Chestnut." She took a deep breath. "Russo had to come get rid of the body after I dragged her in my house and shot her."

I nodded. "Oh yeah, I remember that." I looked at her and kissed her cheek. "You go in the living room and just wipe down everything. I'll take care of all that's in here."

She nodded, kissed me on the lips and walked away.

CHAPTER TWENTY-SEVEN

TAMIKA

"Where have you been?" I asked walking up to Amina when she came in at 1:00 in the morning.

She put her purse on the couch. "Excuse me?"

"I been calling you and—"

"Tamika, I been looking for Russo!" She yelled at me. "Or have you forgotten that nobody has been able to get in contact with my husband."

I took a deep breath. "I'm sorry."

"You don't have to be sorry but you don't have to come at me like that either." She looked around. "Where's Reggie?"

"That's another thing I'm concerned about."

"Why you say that?"

I grabbed her hand and took her to the sofa. "Earlier today I was cleaning the kitchen and to make a long story short, Murphy popped up over here right after I saw something going on in the shed behind the house. When I looked to check it was empty."

Her eyes widened. "What...I mean..."

"What's wrong with you?" It looked like she was about to pass out or something. "Are you okay?"

"Yes...I just...I just need some water." She walked into the kitchen and I followed her.

"Amina, what's going on?" I asked suspiciously.

"Why you keep asking me that?" She yelled. "I already told you that I'm worried about my husband."

"And I get all that. But you also look like you were about to pass out too. I'm just making sure you cool."

She drank a big cup of faucet water from the sink and took a deep breath before turning the water off. "Okay, I feel better now." She paused. "Finish telling me about the shed."

I looked her over and crossed my arms over my chest. When my skin started stinging I dropped them again. "Anyway I think Murphy may have done something to Reggie."

"What? Why?"

"Because the shed was moving and when I left the kitchen to grab my shoes and find out what was up he was at my door."

"Do you really think he's the kind of person to be doing all that?" She asked. "I mean really."

I shrugged. "I don't know."

"Well what happened when you hit Reggie up?"

"No response."

She sighed. "Maybe we should sell this house. It has too much bad energy."

"And go where, Amina?" I yelled.

"I don't know! Anywhere!" She paused and walked out the kitchen. I followed her. "I'm starting to think that Russo was on to something. Apparently a lot of people been hurt by this house and maybe...well maybe it's dragging us down too."

"Nah, we need this house. It's paid off and plus we ain't got no place to go. The little money that we did save up we have to pay for bills and shit like that."

"It was just an idea, Tamika."

"I know." I flopped on the sofa and winced when it stung against my back. "But it was a bad one at that."

She threw her hands up and sat next to me. "I'm out of ideas to tell you the truth. Right now I just wanna take it day by day."

I nodded and looked over at her. "So how are you? Really?" I paused. "With not having Russo around are you lonely?"

"Not really."

I frowned. "Really? Why not?"

"Because me and Russo been disconnected a long time ago. It ain't like we had the dream marriage and for real, all I want now is to make sure he's safe."

"And then what?"

"Once he is then maybe we have to rethink our whole situation."

My eyebrows rose. "You talking about ending your marriage?"

"Like I said, I don't know. But it's a possibility."

"Wow, I don't think I would be able to do that." I paused. "Well...actually, after talking to April it may be worth a try." I took a deep breath.

"Yeah, who would think that she's the one more together than us?"

"But, 'Mina, when you gonna get your baby?" I asked. "Right now April raising her and that ain't a good idea."

She frowned, "Fuck that supposed to mean?"

"Exactly what I said!"

She stood up. "Let me tend to my baby and you tend to your husband."

Now I stood up. "And what is that supposed to mean?"

She stopped at the steps, looked at me and laughed before walking away.

RUSSO

Lying on the floor in the bedroom, sitting in my own shit and piss I decided to do that thing Amina talked about before.

Praying.

"God, I don't know You. I haven't even tried to know You for real because as far as I can see, You never did nothing for me. Well, maybe I wasn't seeing right. But I'm asking You to help me to get out of this before them niggas try and kill me. I don't wanna die. There are so many things I want to do. Like be a father to my daughter and stuff like that. Please. If you there. Help me."

After my prayer I scooted on my stomach to the door. Using as much strength as I had, I leaned on one hand, turned the knob slowly and it was unlocked. Since it was about 4:30 in the morning I figured I could scoot to the front door and get some help. Instead what I saw almost had me yell in happiness.

The nigga Luke was asleep and a stack of mail sat on the recliner along with his cell phone. Slowly I maneuvered toward him careful not to make a sound. And when the floor creaked and he moved, I laid my head down and stayed still.

When I heard him snoring again I crawled some more. First I grabbed a piece of mail and then I grabbed his phone. Quickly but as quietly as possible I maneuvered back to the room and locked the door. It didn't make a difference if I did because they had keys but still.

After I was in the room I leaned against the wall to catch my breath. When I was done I searched my mind for Reggie's number. That's the only downside to programing people's numbers into cell phones. You don't remember numbers when you really need them.

When I finally thought I was good I called him several times. Each time my call went straight to voicemail. "Fuck." I said low.

I didn't remember Amina's number because she got a new phone when she wanted to stop taking calls from Drillo and I couldn't remember none of my nigga's numbers either.

And then it dawned on me. There was one number I did recall. I dialed the digits one by one. When I heard her voice it was the sweetest sound in the world.

"Hello, Mrs. Connelly. It's me. I need some help."

CHAPTER TWENTY-EIGHT

TAMIKA

Lying on my side, I smiled when Reggie crawled up behind me in bed, smelling like soap. He just stepped out of the shower and it felt good to have him next to me, even with my sensitive skin.

"You feel good," I said.

"I'm not too close am I?" He paused. "I'm not hurting you or anything right?"

"I can take a little pain, it means I'm alive." I exhaled. "Just please don't...don't move."

He kissed me on my cheek. "I'm not."

"I had a fight today that I feel guilty about."

"With who?"

"Amina."

He adjusted a little. "What was it about?"

I took a deep breath. "Naverly has been spending a lot of time with April and I...I guess I brought it up and she didn't take it too well."

He exhaled and I looked back at him.

"You okay?" I asked him.

He nodded. "Yes...it's just been a long day and I lost my phone so I been missing out on meetings

BY KIM MEDINA

and stuff for Russo." He paused. "But look, you gotta be careful talking to anybody about their kids. Not everyone is receptive."

"But she's my sister."

"I get that."

"And Naverly's my niece."

"I get that too."

"Well it doesn't sound like it." I turned around and looked at him in the eyes. "Plus she said something that didn't sit right with me. It made me...uncomfortable."

"About what?"

"That I should tend to my husband."

He rolled his eyes. "You know how shit be when you get into a fight with your family. People say all kinds of things they don't mean."

"But it was the way she said it." I paused. "Like she knows something I don't."

"Tamika, you gotta take that up with your sister not me."

"I know." I took a deep breath. "And the last thing I wanna do is fight with you."

"Good, because I'ma be honest, I don't have the energy." He paused. "Not right now."

I nodded. "Yeah, I forget sometimes that you have your own troubles. Your own things that keep you up at night. Like with your mom and stuff like that."

"Yeah, but not really." He shrugged.

I giggled. "What that mean?"

"I have no time for that woman. Zero. I still blame her for half the stuff that's going on around here."

I nodded. "Yeah...but I have to tell you something."

He sighed. "What is it now?"

"She came by the hospital looking for you." I paused. "Well actually she was the one who saved me because Drillo was too high to be any good."

"And you telling this to me because?"

"Because...I don't know...maybe it's time."

"Time for what?" He glared. "To let her back into the picture after all the mental games she's played?"

"I never said that."

"Sometimes I think you get off on having extra drama on your hands."

I frowned. "That's a lie, Reggie."

"Why else would you bring her up when you know how much trouble she's caused you?"

"I don't know. I guess I felt sorry for her that's all." I paused. "And I guess I would want someone to do it for me if I went down that road."

"You did go down that road remember?" He glared. "That's why you on drugs."

"Not really. Like I said this was more Drillo than anything." I took a deep breath.

He smiled and me and shook his head. "I'm only gonna say this once. If you want me in your life don't bring up that bitch's name again." He got out of bed, snatched his robe off the door and stormed out.

CHAPTER TWENTY-NINE

AMINA

I was lying on the sofa crying when I heard the door slam upstairs and Reggie rush down. I sat up, looked at him and lay down again. I could hear his footsteps slapping in my direction.

"What's wrong with you?" He asked me.

I sat up. "I really think something is wrong with Russo."

He nodded and sat next to me. "Me too."

"What do we do?"

"I don't know, Amina. I mean, I did all I could by going to his aunt's house. I even hit up Cambridge but of course that clown's not getting back with me."

"Do you think he hurt him?"

"See that's just it, I don't know what he's capable of." He sighed. "All I know is Russo used to tell me that the nigga was greedy."

"But Russo ain't got no money."

"Russo's version of having no money is different from a lot of people's."

"What that mean?"

He scratched his head. "Amina, how you think we been able to pay the major bills around here and put food in the fridge? Russo tucked away at least $80,000 but he's not gonna give it to no Cambridge either."

I exhaled. "Yeah, I definitely knew he had something tucked away but not that much."

"Yep, and to that dude eighty grand could mean a life change." He paused. "I told him not to trust him but he didn't listen."

"It's a little too late for all that." I exhaled. "Anyway, what you doing down here? You had a fight?"

He looked up the steps and scooted closer. "What you say to her last night?"

I frowned. "Nothing. Why?"

"Did you tell her she needs to tend to her husband?" He whispered.

I smiled. "Yeah, and I'm sorry about that. But she was coming at me about Naverly and this and that. I guess I let my feelings get in the way."

"I don't know what she said to you about Naverly but I do know this, she should be here more. We already dysfunctional enough without having her away from the house. Don't lose your daughter in this shit. You'll hate yourself even more."

I took a deep breath and put my head on the arm of the sofa. "I know."

"So what you gonna do about that?"

"I don't know. Right now I think it's good that April is helping because all I can think about is where Russo is and you. And this thing we have going on."

He looked up the stairs. "I know...when I first came down here I was about to beat my dick but when I saw you were upset I forgot all about it."

Suddenly I was horny. "Can you play in my pussy for a little bit?" I asked him. "Until I cum?"

He bit his lip. "But what about me?" He looked up the stairs and released his dick.

"You can do two at the same time." I put my legs across his thighs and spread them. "Please." I bit my bottom lip.

He pushed back on the top of my pussy with his palm so that my clit popped out. And with his thumb he stroked it softly while I winded my hips. At the same time he beat his dick while I juiced up.

"I love you," I whispered.

"I love you too," he said back.

"Be looking upstairs too." I reminded him when he closed his eyes.

He nodded. "Yeah...yeah...I'ma...I'ma do that." His body tensed and mine did too and within two minutes I came all over his hand and he exploded in his other. With heavy breath I closed my legs sat up and looked at him. He sat on the other end of the sofa and looked at me.

No words.

Just confused silence.

KNOCK. KNOCK. KNOCK.

Reggie got up, lifted the cushion to the recliner across the room, grabbed his gun and tucked it into his robe before looking out the peephole.

"Who is it?" I whispered.

"I don't know." He said. "Some white man."

When I looked behind me Tamika was coming downstairs, also in a robe. "Who at the door?" She asked us.

"We trying to find out now." I told her.

Reggie opened the door and said, "What you want?"

"I'm Peter Lando, Russo's attorney." I stood up and walked toward the door. "Is he here?"

"No but I'm his wife." I responded standing next to Reggie, with Tamika behind me. "What's this about anyway?"

"Well I have some good news. Can I come in?"

I looked at Reggie who nodded, stepped back and allowed him inside. Once in he locked the door. "Have a seat on the couch," Reggie told him.

The lawyer sat down and we all stood around, looking down at him. "Well, it appears that Russo won't be charged after all with the drug possession. The way they entered his home was illegal, so therefore everything after, that came by way of that illegal entry, is what we refer to as *Fruit Of The Poisonous Tree*."

I smiled. "Oh my God."

"So this means no jail time?" Tamika asked, smiling brightly.

"That's exactly what it means!" The attorney said.

We all cheered excitedly. "But what about his house and cars?" Reggie asked.

"Well that's another story. The judge said that as long as he can show legitimate receipts on how he came about the property, it along with the money and cars will be handed over to him. Until then they still hold it all."

194 BY KIM MEDINA

"But that's not right."

"I know...welcome to the government." He put his hand down and quickly pulled it up. "Ew, Uh...something's on my hand." He looked at it closer. "What is this? Cream?"

Reggie moved toward him and wiped his hand quickly by slapping his hand as if he gave him five. "I just had some coffee. Sorry about that."

"Well it was awfully slimy," He continued.

I wanted to look at Tamika but I didn't want to be hot either. What else was creamy and slimy but nut? I could tell Reggie did too but we both continued to focus on the lawyer.

"Well please have him call me when he can. This is great news!" He walked toward the door and then out.

Slowly we both looked at Tamika wondering if she was onto us now.

CHAPTER THIRTY

RUSSO

After I made my call about six hours earlier to Mrs. Connelly I put the phone back and realized how stupid that was. Since I never fucked with the police in any fashion, I didn't even think about calling them when I needed them. And now I realized it was a big mistake. What the fuck did I think Mrs. Connelly was gonna do against Luke's big ass and my cousin?

When I heard keys the door opened. "Any idea on how you gonna get that money?" Luke asked walking inside, with Cambridge behind him.

I wasn't sure but something told me Cambridge wasn't with this crime anymore but now he was in over his head. "Nah."

"Well you know what that mean right?" Luke said. "That means its gonna be a rough night again."

"I'm not getting why ya'll doing all this though." I paused, looking up at them. I could barely see out my eye and my arm still hurt from the fall. "Don't you think if I had some paper I would give it to you? All I want is to be back with my family."

"Nigga, ain't nobody trying to hear that shit," Luke said. "We know you holding something."

"But I'm not!" I said louder.

"Cousin, I know these people," Cambridge said moving closer to me. He squatted down and stared at me. "And he not gonna keep hearing the same shit. It's time to produce the funds."

"You foul. And you better hope if I get out of this that you die right after I do. Because it's gonna be trouble for you."

"But you not going nowhere are you?" He glared.

"I don't know." I shrugged. "We'll see."

"Nigga, you think this a joke," Luke said. "I can already tell." He kicked me in the side.

"Ow!" I yelled, the pain ripping through my body, causing every muscle to tremble.

"Stop all that other shit," Cambridge said. "We ain't gonna get shit if you keep moving like you do."

"But ain't nobody playing with this—

KNOCK! KNOCK! KNOCK!

"What the fuck is that?" Cambridge asked removing his guns from his waist as they both scurried out.

CAMBRIDGE

Cambridge moved toward the door and looked out at three large men wearing black coveralls. He looked at Luke. "You know them niggas," he whispered.

"Nah. I thought you did." Cambridge turned back to the door. "Who you want?"

"I'm here for Russo!" Man #1 said.

Luke looked at Cambridge. "What the fuck? I thought you said nobody knew he was here."

"They didn't," Cambridge said. "I don't know who these niggas are. Never seen them a day in my life."

"Listen, we coming up in there because we know he's there, in a room, in his own shit." #2 said. "Now you can look out of any window you choose and you'll see we got the power and we know you don't. Don't make us blow this bitch down."

Luke looked at Cambridge. "What we gonna do?"

"Don't ask me," Cambridge said stepping back from the door. "This was all on you. I said not to go this far."

Luke and Cambridge rushed to the room where Russo was smiling. "Hey, cousin, who out there?" Cambridge said softly. "You know we were just messing with you right?"

"Yeah...I know that," Russo grinned.

"But why they knocking on the door like they mad and shit?" Luke said just as sweet as a jar of honey. "We wasn't gonna do nothing to you for real."

"What I suggest ya'll do now is open the door." Russo said. "Let's start there."

Fifteen minutes later, after they made Cambridge and Luke wash and clean Russo's ass with their bare hands before putting a fresh diaper on him, Man #1 was carrying him down the steps of the brownstone. Man #2 was carrying the wheel chair. When the fresh air slapped against Russo's face he couldn't believe how grateful he felt.

When he looked back he saw Cambridge and Luke standing at the foot of the steps looking like dead men walking and all Russo could do was grin.

RUSSO

I was sitting in the back of a Black Chevy truck with the whole back seat to myself. "Okay, can ya'll tell me who ya'll are now?" I asked them. "Because I'm definitely grateful."

"We Mrs. Connelly's grandsons."

My jaw hung. "I ain't know Mrs. Connelly had family."

"Yeah, she do." He paused. "We live out here now though. Been in New York for twenty years."

"But why she never said anything about ya'll to me?"

Grandson #1 sighed. "We did some time when we were younger. Some drug shit. Lightweight but a lot of people got hurt and killed, you know." He shook his head. "Even lost a favorite grandson and she never forgave us and for real, I didn't think she would ever talk to us again until now."

"So what made ya'll do this for her?" I paused. "I mean don't get me wrong, I really appreciate it but I didn't expect her to be able to do this. She made it sound like she was about to gas up her car and come get me herself. I had already started feeling bad and everything."

Grandson #2 laughed. "She would have if we let her."

Grandson #1 took a deep breath, "I don't know what her thing is with you but she cares a lot. And I don't have to tell you that you should consider yourself lucky."

CHAPTER THIRTY-ONE

RUSSO

I sat in the tub full of water relaxing. It was weird, I'm not gonna lie how I got in here. Basically one of her grandson's put me in fully clothed and let me get undressed after he left. I tossed the dirty clothes out, turned my water on and Mrs. Connelly came and got my clothes when she heard it running.

Now that I was finished I drained the water out and the same dude put me in the chair after I put on the robe that was sitting on the toilet. I was placed in a soft bed in one of Mrs. Connelly's rooms and I put my own diaper on, slipped on the clean shorts she gave me and a t-shirt.

I felt at peace.

And then I thought about what my cousin did to me. Yeah I had some bread I could get my hands on. But that was for my family, not him. And what does he do? Try to rob and then treat me like shit just because I called him dusty as a kid?

Now I know why nobody messed with him. From D.C. to Baltimore everybody said don't fuck

BY KIM MEDINA

with Cambridge. And I wanted to believe he was changed and look what I get for that?

Nothing!

Knock. Knock. Knock.

I took a deep breath. "Come in."

Mrs. Connelly opened the door, walked over to me and sat on the edge of the bed. "My grandsons are staying a few days. Until it's time for you to leave."

"I can go right now if—"

"Nah...no you won't," she smiled at me. "I can tell when a man needs his spirit re-filled when he's in my presence. I'ma build you back up, as much as I can, and then you'll leave."

I nodded.

"What's going on, son?"

I looked down. "Too much."

She smiled and took a deep breath. "I been seeing a lot of activity over there in the past week or so. Things that don't make me feel so good inside." She put her hand over her chest. "It just makes me feel so...so bad for them. Because I know they mother wanted better instead of the worst."

"What be going on?" I frowned.

"Coming and going. With extreme agitation. Its like, all everybody wants to do is rush and rush and rush." She paused. "You can't have no life like that."

I nodded. "Well I can't do much because, you know, with me in the chair and all."

She laughed.

"What's funny?" I frowned.

"God done already showed me you walking again in my dreams. I saw you with my own eyes. But he has a way of sitting men down a space or two until they can get themselves together."

"Mrs. Connelly, please don't—"

"Now I know you didn't think I saved your life without being prepared to give you a good preaching."

I smiled.

Because as much as she got on my nerves with her God talk I saw the power in it when she had her family save me. And I'm not saying I'm gonna be perfect or not do what I gotta do in the streets but I'm sure if it wasn't for her I wouldn't be here.

"I'm listening."

"You a man. You a married man. And a father too." She said in a low voice. "And married men

BY KIM MEDINA

and fathers need to move like they are carrying the weight of someone else because they are."

"If you talking about Naverly I know," I said. "She my daughter and she gonna always be good."

"I'm talking about your wife too." She paused. "Because based on the bible she comes second only to God."

"You don't know the things she been doing to me."

"I don't. But I can imagine."

"Why you say that?"

"Because you asked to come back to my house instead of going home first." She paused. "Now you a young man. And young men who are held up for a while normally like to do what young men do if you know what I mean." She covered her mouth. "That is, if it still works."

I readjusted a little. "Nah, I'm good down there."

She smiled and it washed away. "Son, you need to slow down. I told you that before but you weren't in a place to receive me. You need to slow down and really look at your surroundings and where you are in life. You need to make decisions that are gonna benefit you and your child and your soul." She paused. "Now I pray for you and that family hard. And when people are prayed on things happen to the level that they need them, to prevent the worst things happening first."

I shook my head. "My cousin tried to kill me."

"Good. Because now you know not everybody is your friend."

"But you don't get it," I said firmly. "I'm from the streets."

"Yeah...yeah...yeah," she said waving the air. "I done heard it all. Don't you see my grandsons downstairs? They told me the same too and a lot of people had to die before they realized ain't no love in the streets. It's bullets or bars that's it!"

"I hear you."

"I hope so, son. Because I don't know how much more time you got if you make a move without thinking."

I nodded. "Thank you."

She touched my leg. "I'm gonna bring you something to eat in awhile."

"I appreciate it. I am hungry."

"I know you are." She walked toward the door but stopped short of leaving. "You can stay as long as you want. Besides, I love having the company and the help from my grandsons around the house." She sighed. "But at some point, Russo. You gonna have to call your wife, hear?"

"Yes, ma'am. I know."

She walked out, leaving me to my thoughts.

CHAPTER THIRTY-TWO
REGGIE

When I saw Amina's car pull up in the parking lot of *Carter's* in White Marsh, Maryland I stood up and waited for her to enter the restaurant. I waved her over and she smiled and walked toward me. She was more refreshed than she had been in the past. Hair done, tight jeans gripped her curves.

The bottom line was she looked beautiful.

"Thank you, thank you for uh...meeting me here." I said. "Figured it would be safer than...you know...after..."

"The attorney had your cum on his hand?" She said.

We looked at each other and broke out into laughter. "Sit down," I said. "Please."

She sat her purse on the table and eased into the seat across from me. For a second I just stared at her. It seemed like as time passed she found beauty in her pain and it made her more appealing. "You are so...so fucking sexy." I took a deep breath.

She shook her head slowly. "Don't...don't do that, Reggie. Please don't do that."

"Do what?"

"I know what this is about." She leaned in closer. "I know so don't play the games."

"Do you really?" I shrugged. "Because I haven't even opened my mouth."

"You're going to tell me that after we almost got caught that made you realize how much you love my sister." She looked down at her fingers. "And how much you don't want your marriage to be over." She shook her head.

"And how much I don't want you to be hurt either, Amina. Because we came dangerously close to losing it all."

"Whatever, Reggie." She waved the air. "I'm not trying to hear all that."

"Whatever?" I repeated more firmly. "If she would've found out that would've meant the end of my marriage but probably the end of your relationship with your sister too. And I don't want that to happen because of me."

"This is so dumb."

"Why?"

"You only doing this because you two have each other but what about me? Who is in my corner?"

"You got Russo."

"Do I?" She asked tilting her head. "You don't want to talk about the possibility that maybe...maybe he's...dead."

"That's not true." I told her.

"But it could be true."

I sat back in my seat and sighed. "We gotta stop."

"Okay."

"Okay what?" I said.

"Okay if you don't want me anymore, we won't do what we do anymore, Reggie."

"So it's that easy for you?" I asked. "Because you giving mixed signals now."

"The only person that's giving mixed signals at this table is you." She said. "But what do you want me to say?"

I looked away from her, at an older couple holding hands at the table across from us. "Maybe you can say something that will make me feel better for breaking your heart."

"I can't do this."

"Do what?"

"Look at you. Knowing that we went there and that I don't want it to end. Even if Russo came back today I want you."

"You're saying that because you're sure he's gone."

"I'm saying that because I'm in love with you, Reggie. And I don't care if you're using me for sex. I don't even care if you don't feel the same. Just don't...don't take yourself away from me right now."

"Fuck, why did I let this go this far?"

"Do you care about me?" She said reaching over and touching my hand. "Because it's simple. If you care about me you won't do this."

"Do what?"

"Cut me off."

I took a deep breath. "I blame myself for this. And I know you don't want to hear it but I will spend the rest of my life proving to you how sorry I am. But I can't leave my wife, Amina. It was never even an option. I told you this." I shrugged. "When we started...when we first got together, I just needed to feel something."

"So you chose me as your rag?" She frowned.

"Is that how you think I think of you?"

She shrugged. "What else am I supposed to think?" She got up and walked away and I followed her.

Bolting out the door she almost got in her car when I grabbed her. "Get off of me, Reggie."

"Not until you give me some more time. I'm not done."

"Get off of me now!"

"No!" I said pulling her into me before kissing her. She wrapped her arms around my neck, her wet tears pressed against my face.

"Don't do this to me, please." She said in heavy breaths. "Don't leave me. Don't do this."

I was about to take her back to my truck when I realized this would be my life forever. Hiding in cracks within our house. Going to restaurants and motels, hoping that nobody would recognize us. And more than anything, the possibility of my wife finding out and being hurt.

So I pushed her away from me. "I'm sorry. But...it's over." I ran to my truck and pulled off.

She dropped to her knees and cried.

CHAPTER THIRTY-THREE

TAMIKA

I was walking down the street to my house, with two grocery bags in my hand when a car pulled up alongside me, scaring me to death. "Hey, don't I know you?" Someone said. "Because I never forget a face."

When I looked over at them I saw it was the guy I gave a lap dance to and shook my head no, before moving faster. I don't even know how he knew it was me. Because of the soft scars and wig. Maybe it was my body. "No, you don't. I...it must be mistaken identity."

"You sure I don't?" He continued to follow alongside me in his car. "Because I can't place the face but you definitely look familiar."

"Look, I already said you don't know me!" I yelled walking faster before rushing up the steps leading to my house. "Now leave me the fuck alone!"

"Fine then," he said before pulling off.

When he was gone I leaned against the door to catch my breath. That's the one thing about living in the streets. When you move fast you wrong a lot of people who don't so easily forget just because you try to go on the straight and narrow.

A little relieved, I pulled out my key and walked into my house and slammed the door, locking it shut. I heard yelling in the kitchen and moved toward the sound, shocked to see Reggie and my sister fighting. He was close to her, as if they were a couple of...a couple of...lovers.

I put the groceries on the table and crossed my arms over my chest. "What could be so serious between you two, that you're arguing like this?" I whispered.

Amina looked at him and then me before walking away without an explanation.

Yeah. Something definitely was up.

I moved closer to Reggie. "Baby, why...why are you fighting with my sister?" My voice high.

He took a deep breath. "No reason."

"Reggie." I said again. "What's going on?"

He sighed. "She wants me to ride down New York looking for Cambridge so he can tell her something about Russo. And I want to stay with you."

Wow.

Relief.

"Well if she wants you to go you should do it."
I exhaled again. "Ain't no need in fighting or
arguing with her at a time like this."

He pulled me toward him. "I know, Tamika."
He separated from me. "But there is a time and a
place for everything and this ain't the time right
now."

I nodded and touched his face. "Are you sure
you okay, Reggie? I feel something is off."

He swallowed. "Yeah, I'm...I'm sure." He
looked over my face and I turned away. "Why you
doing that?"

"Because I don't want you looking at my...the
burns."

"Tamika, trust me, they don't ruin your
beauty at all." He paused. "And even the doctors
said you were lucky so there's that. Trust me. I'm
still very attracted to you."

KNOCK. KNOCK. KNOCK.

Reggie walked past me and toward the front
door. He opened it and on the other side was
April. She looked like she'd been crying.
"Where's...where's Amina." She said walking
inside as if she was breathless.

"I'm right here." Amina said walking down the
steps. "What's going on?"

"There's been...there's been a murder."

"Who?" I asked. "Please don't say, Naverly!"

"Drillo. He was found in a building with a gunshot wound to the head." She said. "He's dead."

I screamed and Amina fell down the stairs.

AMINA

I buried my brother today. It was a no frills type of funeral. The kind they give people who didn't lead a full life or wasn't well loved. And still it was the most painful thing I had ever experienced. Hurt me more than losing my mother, because at least with her I had closure.

Me, Reggie, Tamika, April and Naverly walked back into the house after just getting dropped off by the limousine.

"I'm going to put Naverly to sleep," April said taking her upstairs.

"And I need a nap," Tamika said following her.

Reggie and me were left alone.

"How are you?" He asked looking over at me.

BY KIM MEDINA

I got up and walked to the kitchen. He followed. "You haven't talked to me in a week, Amina. How much longer are you gonna do this?"

"Do what?"

"Ignore me like I'm not here."

"What do you want from me, Reggie?" I asked as a tear rolled down my face. "You said you wanted your space and I gave you that. Just...just let me get over you in peace."

"I never said I wanted my space."

"Correction. You said you didn't want me."

He backed up, leaned against the wall and looked up at the ceiling. "You are torturing me."

"Well just pretend I'm not here. Like when your wife is around. Because the way I feel it's like I don't exist."

"But I can't do that."

"Try." I walked away and out the house.

I had circled the block until I realized I hadn't told Mrs. Connelly about my brother's passing. She wasn't as close to Drillo as she was to us but she'd still care. So I knocked on the door and when someone opened it I was surprised.

He was a large built man with a piece of pie in his hand.

"Hello, is Mrs. Connelly here?"

"Who that...Mrs. C?" A happy voice said from inside. When I saw my husband wheel up to the door, I fainted again.

BY KIM MEDINA

CHAPTER THIRTY-FOUR

AMINA

Russo sat in the living room, in his chair looking at me. "I'm sorry for everything, Russo."

He nodded. "And I'm sorry for what I did to you too." He shrugged. "I will tell you this, I definitely seen a lot differently when I was away. And I want to be different."

I moved closer to the end of the couch so I could see his face clearer. "But why...why stay over there for over a week?"

"Because being around Mrs. Connelly relaxed me."

"And it didn't here?"

He tilted his head and I felt stupid. "You didn't want me here, Amina. And I'm not even saying it's your fault. Its just facts. And I needed to be somewhere where I could get myself together. Mentally and physically."

I nodded. "No. I didn't want you here."

"I get that." He smiled. "But, bae, I...I had a big part in all this shit too." He paused. "I should've never made you feel like it was your fault that this happened to me. And I'm done blaming people for my being in this wheelchair."

"So now you on some positive shit?"

"Ain't saying that." He said seriously. "My cousin did some things that I can't see not dealing with the moment I get right. So revenge is on the mind. But when it comes to me and you I was wrong. I could've been better."

"Me too."

"But I don't know what we gonna do with this marriage, Amina." He said softly. "A lot of hurtful things have been done on both our parts. But I think I wanna try. I think I wanna try not just for myself but for you and Naverly too."

I nodded but looked away. Now that he was here I could tell I had feelings for him but they were nothing like the ones I had for Reggie. "What you think that means, Russo? To try."

He shrugged. "For starters I'm gonna work on myself. Changing up my diet. Getting rid of carbs and sugars and stuff like that. I'm really gonna focus on walking again."

"Really?" I laughed once, trying not to be negative even though I was these days. Once the positive one, I didn't feel like it anymore. "You think your diet gonna work and you gonna be brand new again?"

"Take my shoe off please."

I moved closer and removed one of his shoes. "Now what?"

"Look at my foot."

I looked at his feet and covered my mouth when I saw his toes move. "Oh my God!" I said.

"I'm telling you. It's amazing when you eat right and think right how things be going right."

I was happy for him but a part of me was jealous. While he was over there getting his life right and making decisions to better himself, I was living in a personal hell. One that included loving a man who would never be mine.

I nodded. "That's good, Russo."

He winked. "It is." He took a deep breath. "So what else has been going on? With you."

"You mean besides burying Drillo?"

He shook his head and ran his hand down his face. "I'm sorry. Really sorry that I wasn't here for you."

"You were here," I nodded. "Just not over here." I frowned. "Spent your time with the old bird across the street."

"Hold up. I thought you liked Mrs. C."

"Fuck that bitch," I said.

He blinked a few times. "Who...who are you?" He paused. "You use to be so...so different." He exhaled. "Did I do this to you? Did I...did I turn you into this person?"

I bit my bottom lip.

He nodded. "Okay, well, I sense some anger coming my way. You sure you fine?" He asked.

"No, Russo. I'm not."

"Is there something I could do? I mean, do you want me to go back across the street so you can get yourself together? Maybe be alone?"

I laughed. "You would like that wouldn't you?"

"Why does everything have to be a fight?"

"It's not a fight!" I took a deep breath. "You know what, just do whatever you have to do." I walked away.

REGGIE

I knocked on the back door and walked outside where Amina was sitting on the top step. Russo and Tamika were talking in the front room.

BY KIM MEDINA

"How you doing?" I asked.

"You gonna have to stop doing that." She said to me.

"Doing what?"

"Consoling me. Being there for me. Because all it makes me do is love you even more and that hurts like hell."

"I'm not going to be able to hate you, Amina."

She shook her head. "My life is over, Reggie. Let the dead be."

"It's not," I said. "It's just beginning."

"I won't let you do this you know."

"Do what?"

"I won't let you live happily ever after with my sister." She paused. "You do see that don't you? You are able to understand how much I care and how far I will be willing to go."

I sighed. "I'm afraid of that."

She took a deep breath and looked toward my old house across the yard. Then she looked at me. "I'm prepared right now to offer you your freedom."

"What does that mean?"

"You tell me right now that you don't love me." She paused and I could feel her breath speeding up. "You tell me right now that you can't see touching me, kissing me and holding me anymore and I will leave you alone. I swear I will let you go and move on with my life, starting with moving out and getting my own place." She looked into my eyes. "What is your answer? Do you love me or not?"

I looked at her and looked away. Of course I loved her. That was the problem.

She turned my head and kissed me on the lips. "She can't have you."

TAMIKA

I sat next to Russo and looked at him. Every now and again we would glance over, through the kitchen and out the backdoor at Reggie and Amina who were sitting on the back porch next to one another, way too close for me.

"Russo," I said softly. His eyes were still on them. "Russo, look at me."

He nodded, looked at them once more and back at me. "Yeah...uh...what's...up?"

"I'm not sure because it hurts too much to say but I think they're in love," I said softly. "I...I think..." my voice weighed heavy, like something was pressing on my pipes. Just the thought of them hurting us like this was too much. "I think they may be...having sex."

His jaw dropped. "What...I mean...why...how...how is that possible?" He looked at them sitting on the porch again and back at me. "Are you...are you sure?"

"No I'm not." I shrugged. "But I do know if it happened, it happened when you were held hostage and I was in the hospital because they were all alone. And if that's true, that makes them snakes. The lowest human beings known to man."

Russo was trembling, his jaw tightened and his eyes squinted. "For their sake, I really hope...you lying. I really hope—"

"Russo," A large man said walking up to the opened front door.

I stood up and walked toward it, Russo wheeled himself behind me. "Open the door, Tamika, this is Mrs. Connelly's grandson."

I opened the door and he walked in. "Your new phone is charged up." He said to Russo. "It was

THE HOUSE THAT CRACK BUILT 3   225

going off with back to back messages so Grams told me to bring it over here."

Russo took the phone and hit the button to enter his voicemails. I stood beside him for some reason even though I didn't know why. He pressed a few buttons, put it to his ear and then slowly glared harder than I'd ever seen.

"What's wrong?" I asked. "Who is that?"

"It's a call from Tamara." He looked up at me. "About...about Reggie and Amina."

We both looked at them through the back door. What made it worse was not the news he was about to tell me, but that at no time did they bother to look back at us.

They were brave and bold as they kept each other's company.

Which in my mind meant that they didn't care.

But that would all be changing soon.

COMING SOON

THE HOUSE THAT CRACK BUILT 4: REGGIE & AMINA

228   BY KIM MEDINA

The Cartel Publications Order Form
www.thecartelpublications.com
Inmates **ONLY** receive novels for $10.00 per book.
(Mail Order **MUST** come from inmate directly to receive discount)

Shyt List 1	_____	$15.00
Shyt List 2	_____	$15.00
Shyt List 3	_____	$15.00
Shyt List 4	_____	$15.00
Shyt List 5	_____	$15.00
Pitbulls In A Skirt	_____	$15.00
Pitbulls In A Skirt 2	_____	$15.00
Pitbulls In A Skirt 3	_____	$15.00
Pitbulls In A Skirt 4	_____	$15.00
Pitbulls In A Skirt 5	_____	$15.00
Victoria's Secret	_____	$15.00
Poison 1	_____	$15.00
Poison 2	_____	$15.00
Hell Razor Honeys	_____	$15.00
Hell Razor Honeys 2	_____	$15.00
A Hustler's Son	_____	$15.00
A Hustler's Son 2	_____	$15.00
Black and Ugly	_____	$15.00
Black and Ugly As Ever	_____	$15.00
Year Of The Crackmom	_____	$15.00
Deadheads	_____	$15.00
The Face That Launched A	_____	$15.00
Thousand Bullets		
The Unusual Suspects	_____	$15.00
Miss Wayne & The Queens of DC	_____	$15.00
Paid In Blood (eBook Only)	_____	$15.00
Raunchy	_____	$15.00
Raunchy 2	_____	$15.00
Raunchy 3	_____	$15.00
Mad Maxxx	_____	$15.00
Quita's Dayscare Center	_____	$15.00
Quita's Dayscare Center 2	_____	$15.00
Pretty Kings	_____	$15.00
Pretty Kings 2	_____	$15.00
Pretty Kings 3	_____	$15.00
Pretty Kings 4	_____	$15.00
Silence Of The Nine	_____	$15.00
Silence Of The Nine 2	_____	$15.00
Prison Throne	_____	$15.00
Drunk & Hot Girls	_____	$15.00
Hersband Material	_____	$15.00
The End: How To Write A	_____	$15.00
Bestselling Novel In 30 Days (Non-Fiction Guide)		
Upscale Kittens	_____	$15.00
Wake & Bake Boys	_____	$15.00
Young & Dumb	_____	$15.00
Young & Dumb 2:	_____	$15.00
Tranny 911	_____	$15.00
Tranny 911: Dixie's Rise	_____	$15.00

THE HOUSE THAT CRACK BUILT 3

First Comes Love, Then Comes Murder	_____	$15.00
Luxury Tax	_____	$15.00
The Lying King	_____	$15.00
Crazy Kind Of Love	_____	$15.00
And They Call Me God	_____	$15.00
The Ungrateful Bastards	_____	$15.00
Lipstick Dom	_____	$15.00
A School of Dolls	_____	$15.00
Hoetic Justice	_____	$15.00
KALI: Raunchy Relived	_____	$15.00
Skeezers	_____	$15.00
You Kissed Me, Now I Own You	_____	$15.00
Nefarious	_____	$15.00
Redbone 3: The Rise of The Fold	_____	$15.00
The Fold	_____	$15.00
Clown Niggas	_____	$15.00
The One You Shouldn't Trust	_____	$15.00
The WHORE The Wind		
Blew My Way	_____	$15.00
She Brings The Worst Kind	_____	$15.00
The House That Crack Built	_____	$15.00
The House That Crack Built 2	_____	$15.00
The House That Crack Built 3	_____	$15.00

(**Redbone 1** & **2** are **NOT** Cartel Publications novels and if **ordered** the cost is **FULL** price of $15.00 each. **No Exceptions**.)

Please add $5.00 **PER BOOK** for shipping and handling.

The Cartel Publications * P.O. BOX 486 OWINGS MILLS MD 21117

Name: _____

Address: _____

City/State: _____

Contact/Email: _____

Please allow 5-7 BUSINESS days before shipping.

The Cartel Publications is NOT responsible for Prison Orders rejected, NO RETURNS and NO REFUNDS.

NO PERSONAL CHECKS ACCEPTED

STAMPS NO LONGER ACCEPTED

BY KIM MEDINA

Made in the USA
Columbia, SC
19 January 2018